Finding a Bride

R.J. Groves

Copyright © 2018 by R.J. Groves
Edited by Graham Toseland. www.fadingstreet.com
ISBN: 978 0 6452675 6 3
Groves Publishing
Formats available: eBook, Paperback

About the author

Australian author R.J. Groves has been passionate about writing since she could put pen to paper and can usually be found jotting plots and stories down on anything she can get her hands on. Describing herself as a mum, wife, author, and coffee lover, her other passions include music, cooking, books, adventures, and searching for plot bunnies in even the most mundane activities.

Facebook: facebook.com/rjgauthor
Instagram: instagram.com/r.j.groves_author
Twitter: twitter.com/rjg_author
Website: www.rjgrovesauthor.com

Books by R. J. Groves

The Bridal Shop series
Save the Date
Be My Valentine
Say You'll Be Mine

Jilted Brides series
Finding a Bride
Written in the Sand

Cities of the World series
In Paris
The Irish Maiden

Set Ups series
The Set Up

Mail Order Brides series
The Calm in the Storm

The Warmth in the Winter
The Song in the Silence

Standalones
Writing You
Two Babies Too Many
Second Chance
The Boyfriend Application
Sweeter Things
Home Bound
Stay With Me
Her First Noel
When Dreams Come True
To Fall For You

To all my Elsewhere friends for your support, encouragement, and undying readiness to war.

Finding a Bride

R.J. Groves

Chapter 1

'Any progress?'

Axel rubbed his temple. 'Nothing,' he said. After studying for so long to get his law degree, he thought he should have been an expert at finding information by now. He never figured that he'd be presented with a bulletproof case and be expected to find a way to bring them down. Sure, he'd only recently graduated and had only just started this job working for Cameron Landon, but he was a qualified lawyer now. And a lawyer needs to find the loopholes in any case, regardless of how bulletproof it appeared to be.

'Damn it.' Cameron sat next to him. 'Have you had a look through their financial records to find any discrepancies?'

'Not yet,' Axel said. Honestly, he hadn't even thought about it.

'Why don't you take a break, then,' Cameron said, taking the papers out of Axel's hands and handing him a bank note. 'Get us some coffees and breathe some fresh air, and I'll see what I can find.'

Axel took the note and headed towards the door. 'Flat white?' he asked.

'Extra strong.' Cameron continued studying the papers.

The crisp fresh air hit Axel like it was the first time he'd stepped outside. He knew he had to have his head buried in the books while studying, but never imagined he would still have to do it every day of his career. Why hadn't anyone warned him out about that? University had been daunting enough for him. He'd only ever been told that being a lawyer is a fast-paced profession with many rewards and that he would love it. Sure, it was fast-paced … to a deadline, that is. And without a doubt, he got an adrenaline rush whenever he was in the courtroom. But he could do without the intense research and late nights. And sure, it paid well. Or, it would, when he finished his graduate year. Maybe then he could buy himself a decent suit.

He took a deep breath and headed towards the café a couple blocks down from the office. Cameron's suggestion of *extra strong* sounded pretty good.

*****

She looked like a princess. She felt like a princess. Everything Caitlyn had ever dreamed of was coming true—a perfect man, a perfect wedding, a perfect life—and it was all only a few days away. She clutched her stomach. Already the jitters were coursing through her. She was excited and scared at the same time for how her life would be different. She would no longer be Miss Caitlyn Low, but Mrs Caitlyn Graeme. She twitched her nose. The name would take some getting used to. She'd always liked her last name, and she still wasn't convinced that Graeme would be an improvement, but she loved Andy, and it was a small sacrifice for the life he could offer her—travel, family, security. She would have to get used to it.

'All right, you're done. You can get dressed now.'

She stepped down off the small stage in front of the full-length mirror. 'Is the dress ready?' she asked, allowing the dressmaker to pull the wedding dress back over her head and putting her own clothes back on.

'A few minor adjustments, but it will be ready for you to pick up tomorrow, along with the bridesmaid's dress.'

'We'll be here,' Sophia said, passing Caitlyn her handbag.

Sophia had been Caitlyn's best friend for as long as she could remember. They had always done everything together and were closer than sisters. Even when they fought, they quickly made up.

Caitlyn was sure that Sophia wasn't happy about her and Andy at first. She knew that Sophia had been crushing on Andy even when they were in school, but Caitlyn and Andy were as close to an arranged marriage as they could get. They had been pressured by their families to start dating and, well, they eventually fell in love in time to be married. Sophia had never let on that she still may have feelings for him. It was a long time ago now, anyway, and it was an issue that had long been resolved. Besides, Sophia had jumped at the opportunity to be Caitlyn's maid of honour and couldn't be more thrilled about it.

'So, only two more days. Are you excited?' Sophia asked, linking her arm through Caitlyn's.

'It's hard not to be,' Caitlyn said.

They started walking towards the little café down the street that had become their habit after dress fittings—for skinny latte's and a low-carb, low-sugar slice at the most since Caitlyn had a perfect white dress to fit into.

'I don't know, Soph. Seeing myself in that dress— it felt so perfect, so real. It feels like I've waited so long for this day and now it's so close I can feel it in my veins.'

'Honey, you *looked* perfect in that dress,' Sophia said. 'I swear, if you didn't buy it, I would have and saved it for my wedding day.'

Caitlyn laughed. 'Now, we just need to find you a man.'

They reached the café in high spirits, Caitlyn pirouetting excitedly before flinging the door open and colliding with a brick wall. Or that's what she thought it was, until the wall cursed, and she realised she'd bumped into a man and spilled his coffees all over his shirt.

'Seriously?' he said, putting what was left of the coffees on a nearby table and started dabbing at the stain with a handful of napkins.

'You should really watch where you're going.' She moved around him to catch his eyes. If there was one thing she'd learned about etiquette, it was to always make eye contact when you're talking to someone. That way, you can sense their emotions and they will see how confident you are.

'*I* should watch where *I'm* going?' He span, staring right at her, his eyes blazing.

God, he was taller than she'd first thought—a good head taller than her. And his russet-brown hair was neatly cut. She could feel his steel-grey eyes boring through her, and his lips were curled, halfway between a mocking smile and a snarl. The faint, woody scent of his cologne was tinted with the smell of coffee and it took her breath away. She could feel her confidence fading.

'You're the one who came barging through the door, spilling my coffees, and ruining my suit.' He gestured with his arms to exaggerate his point.

'Pirouetted,' she said, holding her finger up in front of her.

'What?'

'I didn't barge, I pirouetted,' she repeated. He stared blankly at her. 'You know, twirled? Danced?'

'Well, here's an idea,' he said, through gritted teeth, 'keep your superfluous frolicking to yourself.' He dabbed at his shirt, cursing again when his efforts were useless.

'*Superfluous frolicking?*' she repeated.

Whoever this man was, he was getting under her skin, and she didn't like it. He dropped his head backwards, staring at the ceiling for a second, before turning back to her.

'What, you're not finished yet?' he asked flatly.

'You can't just insult me and expect that to be the end of the conversation,' she said.

She poked his chest, then clutched her finger with her other hand. So, she hadn't been exaggerating when she'd thought she'd hit a brick wall, since his chest was about as hard as one. He raised an eyebrow.

'What's the matter, princess?' he said, his lips curving into that snarl again. 'Can't take your own medicine?'

She squinted, her blood boiling. 'Princess? Why, you little—'

'I'm sorry,' Sophia said to him, grabbing Caitlyn by the arm in an attempt to diffuse the situation. 'She's getting married in two days and we just had our final dress fitting.'

'Oh, well, that explains it,' he said, his tone dripping with sarcasm. 'I'll just let you off the hook for ruining my suit.'

'Shirt,' Caitlyn said.

'What?'

'Your suit is fine. It's your shirt that's stained.'

He shook his head. 'You know, I pity your fiancé. Someone should tell him what he's in for.'

'Excuse me?'

'Buy me another one.'

'Buy you a suit?' She almost laughed out loud.

'A coffee, since you spilled mine,' he said, squinting at her. 'I wouldn't trust you to buy me a suit.'

'Where are your manners?' she said, hands on hips.

'Probably out the door with yours,' he said, obviously doing his best to stay calm.

She'd just about had it with this man, whoever he was. He made her so angry. He annoyed her and made her skin prick. She briefly felt that she'd met her challenge. He was witty and sarcastic. He made her feel empowered and vulnerable at the same time. And she couldn't think clearly around him. She dug through her purse, pulling out a handful of coins and plonked them on the table next to his cups.

'Knock yourself out,' she said, taking Sophia by the arm and beelining towards a table.

'Thank you, *so* much, for your generosity.' He bowed deeply.

She could feel every inch of her body shaking as she took a seat. How had she gone from being on top of the world to being so furious at a stranger? She'd never met anyone in all twenty-six years of her life who made her feel like he did in a matter of minutes. She closed her eyes and took a deep breath. She would never see this arrogant bastard again and, in two days, she would be happily married to Andy and this incident would be well and truly forgotten. She smiled. Two days.

***

Axel walked quickly. He had already been gone longer than he should have—Cameron would be wondering where he was. But he'd had to take a lap around the block to get that woman out of his head. Who did she think she was, talking so rudely to someone she hadn't met before when she was the one that knocked into him? Not to mention that she'd wrecked his best shirt. It was like the icing on the cake. The sour icing on the terrible, spoiled cake that was his day. His day was already bad enough. Now, this?

He'd watched her hyacinth eyes turn into a violet flame and her ash-brown bob jiggling throughout their dispute. He would have forgiven her if she hadn't told him to watch where he was going. He knew her character well. She was insecure, vulnerable, apprehensive. Or, so he thought, until she showed him her arrogant side in her abrupt and snide way of talking. He couldn't help throwing it back at her. He smiled as he pictured the face she pulled when he called her pirouette *superfluous frolicking*. He knew what a pirouette was—his sister had many years of ballet lessons when they were growing up. What baffled him is why she would be pirouetting into a café without looking.

He frowned. He didn't know what made him call her *princess*. The only person he has ever exchanged insults and names with was his sister, and he'd never called her *princess* before. Maybe saying that he pitied this woman's fiancé was a bit harsh, but it flew out of his mouth before he could stop it. He could still smell the sweet scent of apple and cinnamon that hit him when she poked him. Truth is, she made his blood boil and aroused his sensations at the same time. Yet, he couldn't help but feel that his sarcasm had a hint of flirting with it, no matter how much he tried to subdue it.

He fingered one of the coins that she gave him and pulled it out of his pocket. He hadn't realised until he left the café that one of them was an old metal token. It obviously meant nothing to her, since she tried to pass it off as a coin, but he found it fascinating. It reminded him of an old slot-machine token. He turned it over and read the print on the back, *The Grand Casino*. This woman was someone else's problem. Her friend said that she would be married in two days. Hopefully, he'd never see that beautiful, arrogant woman again. Flirting with a married woman was something he was not accustomed to doing, but he wouldn't be able to help himself.

He tucked the token back into his pocket and opened the door to the office. Cameron looked up from his work and furrowed his brow, taking one of the coffees from the cup tray as Axel placed it on the desk.

'What happened to you?' He pointed at the stain on Axel's shirt.

'Long story,' he said, taking the seat opposite Cameron, and sipping his coffee. He proceeded to tell him about his interaction with the soon-to-be-married woman—the short version, leaving out the fact that he had considered kissing her only a second before her friend said that she was getting married.

Cameron laughed and pulled a fresh shirt out of one of his drawers and handed it to Axel.

'Word of advice,' he said, 'you should make sure you always have a few fresh shirts at the office. You never know when someone might throw something in your face.'

Axel smiled. 'Speaking from experience?'

'Possibly,' Cameron said.

'What do you do when that happens?'

Cameron smiled. 'Change your shirt and send them the dry-cleaning bill.'

Chapter 2

'Caitlyn, there's someone here to fill a prescription.'

Caitlyn looked up from her inventory notes to Jake. She'd always wanted to be a pharmacist from the first moment she studied an introduction to medical science, but working the late shift wasn't her first choice. Though, she had grown used to working with Jake as her chemist assistant.

'Just a minute,' she mumbled.

She had to finish her inventory before she lost count—it was the last thing she had left to do on her last day of work before getting married and leaving for her honeymoon. She'd put in for a month of leave and would be enjoying every second of it. When she started back at work, she might convince them to switch her to the day shift, since she would no longer be considered a single person. She laughed, highly doubting that it would happen. But it didn't hurt to dream, right? She kept counting—almost there.

'Caitlyn!'

'I'm coming,' she said, officially losing count. 'Damn it, Jake, didn't I say not to interrupt me when I'm doing inventory?'

'Well, I can't help it if someone comes in right before we close, wanting to fill a prescription,' he said.

'Can't you do it?' She followed him out from the back, already knowing the answer.

'Not qualified yet.'

'How long to go?' she asked.

'About two months,' he said, a wide grin on his face.

'I think I'm going to miss having you as my assistant,' she said, frowning and sticking out her bottom lip.

'You'll just have to treat me as your equal,' he said, then indicated to the desk. 'Here you are.'

'How can I help?' she said, smiling at their customer.

The tall man looked up from a pamphlet he was holding and dropped it onto the counter, his mouth falling open. The smile on her face fell quicker than she'd put it on.

'You,' she said.

The man from the café. The customer was the rude, sarcastic, name-calling, incredibly attractive man from the café whose coffee she accidentally spilled on his shirt. He pointed towards the door, clutching his prescription in his hand.

'I can go somewhere else,' he said.

A loud laugh escaped, and she clamped her hand over her mouth. He raised an eyebrow. Caitlyn cleared her throat.

'Well, good luck finding another chemist open this late,' she said.

'I can wait until the morning.'

'Is that why you're in here at ten minutes to midnight?' she asked.

He tapped his fingers on the bench. 'Like I said, I can wait until the morning.'

***

It must be just his luck to walk into the chemist where she worked. She had never struck him as a pharmacist. Honestly, he didn't think she even had a job. She had that rich privileged persona going on. He figured that the man she was marrying must be well set up and could provide for her while she played house. But here she was, working a late shift in the only chemist that was open until midnight— he'd googled it.

'Well, you're here, so you may as well let me fill it,' she said, snatching the prescription slip from his hands.

'Hey!' he said, trying to snatch it back. She held it out of reach.

'It's not like I'll mess it up because you were being a jerk today,' she said, reading through. 'Let's see what we have.'

He felt his body heating up. He couldn't believe that she had managed to get hold of the prescription. The whole point of going to the chemist so late at night was to avoid being seen by anyone he knew or planned on ever seeing again. After all, the only person who knew he was on any kind of medication was his sister. He swallowed, watching her as her eyes scanned the print. Her brow furrowed, and she looked back up at him.

'These are antidepressants,' she stated, matter-of-factly. 'I'm sorry, I didn't know.'

'I'm not depressed,' he said defensively. 'They're to help me deal with stress.'

Not that he had to justify himself to this woman. But, for some reason, he felt that, at the very least, he couldn't have her pitying him. It wasn't a lie. He wasn't depressed, nor did he have the tendency to be. He was apprehensive to take antidepressants at first, or any kind of medication, for that matter. But the doctor said that, if he took them on an as-needed basis, it would help him with his stress. It started when he was in university—study always made him stressed, particularly before exams—and continued when he started working at the office. He refused to take them all the time, but there were some days that were particularly stressful. Today was one of them and it just so happened that he'd run out of his pills, meaning that he'd had to find a chemist that was open, since his usual chemist was already closed.

'Still, I didn't know,' she repeated.

'It's not exactly something I advertise,' he said, his voice low.

A faint smile crossed her lips. 'Give me five minutes and I'll have it ready for you,' she said.

He watched as she walked out the back before taking a seat near the counter. The last thing he wanted was her pitying him, but it was all over her face. Not to mention that he never thought he'd see her again, but now he'd seen her twice in one day. It shouldn't matter what she thought of him. Though, he couldn't help but feel something—he didn't know what. She made him furious. Saying that he was acting like a jerk? If only she could see how she was acting. He couldn't stand her. But her slim figure, attractive looks and sweet smell still got to him. And maybe her fiery temper could keep things interesting. But she would soon be married to someone else and, now, she pitied him. That was enough to deter him.

***

'Do you know that guy?' Jake asked, his voice only a little above a whisper.

Caitlyn glanced up from measuring the dosage and nodded slightly before shrugging. 'I spilled his coffee over his shirt this morning,' she said. Jake's eyes widened. 'It was an accident,' she continued. 'I was excited after the dress fitting and didn't look where I was going and bumped into him. I freaked out, said something I probably shouldn't have, and things escalated from there.'

'You kissed him?'

'No, we didn't kiss,' she said. 'We argued. I didn't think I'd ever see him again.'

'But you wanted to kiss him,' Jake said, nudging her arm.

'What? I—' She felt a blush creeping into her cheeks. Did she? She cleared her throat. 'I'm getting married, Jake, in two days. I am already living with Andy and I'm not that kind of girl.'

'But you still wanted to kiss him,' he repeated. 'And you're not married, yet.'

'You know, I think your shift is over. You should really get back home to that girlfriend of yours.'

His face dropped. 'You don't want me to stay until you're finished?' he asked.

She shook her head, putting the pills in a container and writing his name on the container. *Axel Taylor*. 'I still have to finish inventory,' she said. 'But there's no point keeping you here for longer than you'll be paid for.'

'Point taken,' he said, logging off on his time card. 'Oh, and you might be interested to know that I overheard this guy giving advice to someone at the café the other day.'

Her eyes widened. 'So, he likes putting in his two cents' worth—doesn't everyone?'

Jake shook his head. 'He wasn't just voicing his opinion,' he said. 'He was giving them legal advice.'

Her breath caught. 'You mean—'

'He's a lawyer, Caitlyn,' he said, pulling his coat on. 'So maybe be careful about what you say to him. You wouldn't want to piss him off, especially with how public a figure Andy is.'

Andy was a whole different suit altogether—running for council and aspiring to become the Mayor of Goulburn. He was smart, sophisticated, and well-to-do, so much so that his father wanted them to sign a pre-nuptial agreement in case they didn't work out. Considering that their whole union was practically planned by their parents since she and Andy were kids, she thought there would be no need for such a contract, but obliged anyway.

She watched as Jake left, wondering if she had possibly been a bit rude to this guy—Axel, according to his prescription. After all, if he truly was a lawyer and felt like stirring up trouble to get back at her for being so abrupt with him, it wouldn't take much effort to find how to do it. With Andy hoping to become Mayor, all it would take was a lawsuit leaked to the public to make people start questioning his suitability. They were already trying to keep a lawsuit quiet from the press for some shady business that his father had been involved with some time back. She took a big breath and headed towards the front to give him his prescription. He obviously already didn't like her, so now she just had to make sure that things didn't escalate. Again.

'Here you are, Mr Taylor,' she said.

***

He raised his eyebrows, his expression shocked. 'Mr Taylor?' How did she know his name?

'That is your name, right?' she asked. 'Axel Taylor?'

'Yes, but—' he said, his eyes questioning.

'On your prescription,' she explained. 'I had to write your name on the bottle.'

'You seem to be at an advantage then, since I don't know your name,' he said, taking the bottle of pills from her outstretched hand.

She hesitated for a moment before replying. 'Caitlyn.'

Caitlyn. A name he had always thought sounded nice, sophisticated, sweet. Now, as he looked at her, he could see that she was a Caitlyn, even after their earlier argument had escalated. She'd confused him more than a woman had ever confused him before. She was everything fury—furious, infuriating. Fury by its very definition. Yet, he'd still felt that she was damn near irresistible.

'Well, Caitlyn,' he said, 'I couldn't have pictured you as a pharmacist until now.'

'What did you think I was?' she asked, her eyebrow raised.

'I don't think you would want to know,' he replied.

He figured she probably wouldn't want to know that he thought that she was rich, privileged, and marrying for money. Caitlyn scowled, and he briefly wished he could wipe the frown from her face. She looked prettiest when she smiled, even if it was a fake, pity-filled smile. But she was someone else's.

'Well, I couldn't have pictured you as a lawyer, but here we are,' she spat, her tone fuelled with fire—the Caitlyn that he'd had the most experience with.

'How the hell do you know that?' he asked.

He could feel his skin pricking. Who was this woman? She'd managed to find out his secret, his name, and now his career without him telling her any of it. And all he knew about her was where she worked and her first name.

'My assistant recognised you,' she said, crossing her arms over her chest. 'Tell me, is it a good feeling spending your time finding ways to make sure that someone loses everything?'

'That's not fair,' he said. Caitlyn was back to being furious again, but he couldn't understand how she could be furious about his career. 'I studied for years to become a lawyer. You have no right to shut it down.' He put the money for the pills on the bench and started to head towards the door. 'You know, it's people like you that caused me to need this damn medication to start with.'

'You should be thanking me for filling your prescription so late at night.'

Axel turned to face her. He should be thanking her? The only thing he should be thanking her for is the headache she has given him.

'Well, it is your job, after all,' he said. 'But, you know, I could always sue you if you turned me away.'

He watched the smug look fall from her face and her mouth opened and closed a few times before closing into a tight line. He'd hit a nerve—he could tell. If there was one thing he'd become good at with being a lawyer, it was identifying the exact moment that someone realised they were fighting a losing battle. But what intrigued him was how easily she got that look which meant one thing. She was scared of being sued. She had either been put through the wringers before, or had a reputation to think of that would be tainted by a lawsuit.

'But as seems to be customary for us,' he said, his hand on the front door. 'Thank you, again, for your generosity.'

Chapter 3

Caitlyn blinked up at the ceiling. After finally finishing inventory the night before, she had officially started her leave from work. And she would be getting married tomorrow. God, it felt so surreal. She couldn't believe she had been so excited yesterday as though she'd thought her wedding day would never come, and now she couldn't believe that it was only a day away.

She could see the pattern starting on the walls from the first morning sunlight shining through the lace curtains. She might have still been excited, had she not met Axel Taylor. But, in the course of a day, he'd got inside her head and messed with her sleep. She'd come across many strange characters working as a pharmacist, especially on the late shift. But she'd never been threatened with a lawsuit there before. Had he meant what he said? Would he have sued her if she turned him away? Why couldn't she just keep her mouth shut?

There was something about Axel that seemed to bring out the worst in her. She knew that she shouldn't let him get under her skin. Sure, she'd seen him twice in one day. But, she'd probably never see him again. Part of her was disappointed. She couldn't stand to be near him, but she still couldn't get him out of her head. She'd wondered, briefly, if there had been a hint of flirting in his sarcasm, but felt bad for even thinking it. She was to be married—*tomorrow*—and definitely wasn't the kind of person to cheat on her husband, especially when she had everything she'd ever wanted. So, why did she feel like there was still something missing?

Was her mind already cheating by being occupied of thoughts of another man, even though they weren't romantic thoughts? Well, most of them. She had, admittedly, wondered what it would feel like to kiss him. And she did know that, in the best romance stories, their exact situation with the addition of a kiss mid-argument would make for a good tale to tell. Maybe it was the pre-wedding jitters. Or maybe it's because she had never been with another man except for Andy. She'd never experienced the heartbreak of losing a first love or the feeling of realising that everything she ever wanted was right there in front of her.

Her whole life, she had done as she was told. Her life was planned by her parents, structured—everything except for her job, which her parents figured was only temporary. Her mother had always said that it didn't matter what she did for a job because, once she was married, she would be starting a family and looking after kids instead of working. She'd gone along with it, revelling in the fact that it was one area of her life that she could decide on for herself. Now, she wasn't so sure she was ready for kids and she certainly wasn't ready to leave work. But the time had come. They had held off on getting married so that she could finish her degree and work for a couple of years. Andy had already waited for her, it would be selfish to make him wait longer.

'Are you okay, babe?'

Caitlyn turned in the bed to face Andy. How long had he been watching her? She hadn't even noticed him stirring. Things would be good with Andy. She should feel lucky that she never had to go through heartbreak. Things with Andy were comfortable, secure. And she was sure that they would have some exciting times where she could feel the thrill of living. They just had to get past the election. She may not agree with everything he wanted for the town, but she had to support him.

She nodded. 'Just thinking,' she said. 'I couldn't get to sleep.'

He pulled her into his arms and she snuggled against his chest—even his scent seemed mundane and comfortable, unlike the faint woody smell of Axel's cologne that excited her and scrambled her thoughts. She wondered what it would be like to get to know Axel. At least they already fought like there's no tomorrow. She couldn't even remember if her and Andy had fought—their heated discussions were more like debates rather than arguments. At least she'd know that things would always be interesting with Axel and, from what she'd heard, a good fighter was often a better lover.

She felt her body stiffen and scolded herself for thinking about—comparing, rather—another man while in the arms of her fiancé. Her wondering wouldn't matter, anyway. Hopefully, she'd never see Axel again and she could just focus on her and Andy. It was absurd even wondering what it would be like to be with Axel. Even if she wasn't engaged, or with Andy, she obviously would never have a chance with him—you have to at least be able to get along to start a relationship.

'Anything in particular?' he asked, his eyes closed.

'Just nerves,' she lied. Andy didn't know about her confrontation with Axel and she planned to keep it that way.

Andy's alarm went off and he eased out of bed. Caitlyn propped herself up on an elbow.

'You're getting up now? It's still early, isn't it?' she asked.

'We're planning on settling so that the lawsuit doesn't reach the public eye,' he explained, pulling his trousers on and buttoning his shirt. 'I have to meet with the lawyer and my father to decide how much we'll offer. You were late coming home last night. Was everything okay at work?'

She scratched her head. 'Everything's fine,' she said. 'I just had to finish inventory before leaving. I'm still sure it won't get done again until I go back, so I wanted to do a good job of it.' She didn't want to tell him that she kept losing count because Axel had invaded her mind.

'I thought you weren't going back,' he said, tying his tie around his neck and straightening it.

She sat up, frowning. 'It was always my intention to go back, Andy,' she said. 'You know that. I've worked too hard for it to just give it up as soon as we're married.'

He waved his hand at her. 'We can talk about it when we get back from our honeymoon.'

'My intentions are still going to be the same then, Andy,' she said, pressing her palm to her forehead.

He turned to face her and smiled. 'We'll see,' he said, then left without another word.

She groaned, letting herself drop back against the bed. She didn't have any appointments until the afternoon, so she may as well try to get at least some sleep before her big day.

***

'My client wants to settle.'

Axel watched the exchange between Cameron and the defending lawyer. Cameron tapped his fingers on the table.

'What's he offering?' Cameron asked.

The other lawyer, Derek Small, a stout man with a neatly combed moustache who looked like he didn't lift more than the pen he was holding, pulled out a cheque and slid it across the table. Without touching it, Cameron read the figure and shook his head.

'Not a chance,' he said.

'You have an obligation to present it to your client,' the stout man said.

'I'll present it to him. But I can tell you now that my client will say the same thing,' Cameron said. 'Though, he'd probably include a few more choice words than I did.'

Derek's moustache twitched. 'This is the last chance to settle before it goes to trial,' he said.

Cameron pushed the cheque back to Derek. 'Then, we'll see you there.'

They all rose to their feet and Derek left quicker than he came in. Axel turned to Cameron.

'That was a lot of money you just turned down,' he said.

'Yes, it was,' Cameron said, smiling.

'Are you sure he would have turned it down?'

'Positive,' Cameron said, heading towards his desk. 'People don't offer to settle unless they have something to hide. Besides, our client isn't looking for money. He wants to see Andy Graeme fall.'

***

'Tash, I'm home,' Axel said.

He closed the front door behind him and dropped his keys and wallet into the bowl on the hall table as Flop, his terrier, greeted him. He scratched Flop on his tummy. Tash sat up from lying down on the couch and looked at him.

'So, I have good news and bad news,' she said. 'What do you want first?'

'Good news.'

'I got the coffee stain out of your shirt,' she said, putting her finger up in front of her. 'But before you get too excited, your pale blue shirt now has a massive bleach stain on it, so it's no good anyway.'

'You used bleach on my shirt?' he asked. Now he would have to buy a new shirt to replace it. *Damn*. At least it was the weekend now, so he could go to the shops. 'You said I could trust you with it.'

'How was I supposed to know it would stain your shirt more than the coffee did?'

'You only use bleach on whites, Tash.' He hung his suit jacket over the back of one of the dining chairs. 'Speaking of coffee, did I tell you that the coffee girl was at the chemist last night?'

'No, I haven't seen you since you left,' she said. 'What was she getting?'

'Not getting,' he said, walking towards his room, and pausing at the door. 'Working. She's a pharmacist. She filled my prescription. Her name's Caitlyn, by the way.'

'How'd that go for you?' She raised her eyebrow.

He smiled. 'Much like the coffee experience.'

She laughed. 'I don't know why you take those pills, anyway. There are other ways to destress yourself.'

'Getting laid isn't really an option at the moment.'

'I wasn't talking about getting laid, you idiot,' Tash said, throwing a cushion at him.

'Well, I already take Flop for runs,' he said, shrugging. 'But in answer to your question—you, my dear sister, your crazy antics, and your on-again off-again relationship with Liam are the reason I'm on medication.' He smiled a cheeky grin as Tash squinted at him.

'It's why you love me,' she said.

'You drive me insane,' he joked. Much like Caitlyn had.

He went to his room, Flop at his heels, and plugged his phone into the charger near his bed, picking up the metal slot token that Caitlyn had tried to palm off as a coin. He turned it over in his hand a few times before putting it back down on the bedside table.

***

Caitlyn blinked at herself in the mirror. It was happening. It was really happening. Her big day was finally here. She should be excited. She was nervous, but not excited.

'It has to be the dress,' she said, tugging at the layers of material.

'The dress is perfect,' Sophia said.

'My hair?'

'Also, perfect,' Sophia said. 'Everything is perfect.'

'Then, what's missing?' she asked.

'Nothing is missing, Caitlyn. You're just having a pre-wedding freak out.'

Caitlyn shook her head. 'No, if I was having a pre-wedding freak out, I would be running around like a crazy person,' she said. 'Something is missing.'

Was she having a meltdown? Surely, not. Like she said, she would be running around like a crazy person. So, what was it? She still loved Andy, and she *did* still want to marry him, even if Axel had briefly taken over her thoughts. God, she wished her grandfather was there. He would have known what was missing. She was convinced that he knew everything.

'Well, it's nothing to do with how you look,' Sophia said, studying her with her hand on her chin. 'You even have something old, something new, something borrowed, and something blue.'

Old. Why hadn't she thought of that before? 'That's it!' she yelled, racing to her bag.

Her grandfather couldn't be here to see her get married, but she had something that made her feel like he was. She rummaged through her bag and pulled out her purse, opening up the coin pocket, then searching through every other pocket before emptying out her bag.

'Where is it?' she said, her voice shaking.

God, she couldn't have lost it. She'd carried it around in her purse for twelve years—since she'd said her goodbyes to him on his deathbed. She could feel her eyes welling up. It wouldn't be right without it. It wouldn't be right without *him*.

'Caitlyn, calm down,' Sophia said. 'Tell me what you're looking for.'

'The slot-machine token!' she said, almost yelling. She held her hands to her temples. 'Oh, God, I can't find it.'

'Your grandfather's token?' Sophia asked, her face paling. Sophia knew how much that token meant to her.

'*Yes*!'

'I'm sure it will be here somewhere,' Sophia said, helping her look.

They spent a few minutes tearing everything out of her bag, searching pockets, and even searching under the chairs in the bridal room with no luck. With every passing second, she could feel her heart sinking further.

'It's not here, Soph,' she said, a tear squeezing out.

'It'll show up, I'm sure of it,' Sophia said. 'It probably fell out at home. But you know that your grandfather is always here with you, Caitlyn.' She pressed a finger to Caitlyn's chest. 'With or without the token.'

Caitlyn flopped down onto one of the seats, resting her head in the palms of her hands. 'I know,' she said. 'But still.'

'Why don't I go ask Andy if he has it?'

'Would you? Please?'

'I'll be back soon.'

Caitlyn wiped the tear away as she watched Sophia leave. She knew that her grandfather was always with her in her heart, but that token was still the only thing of his that she had. She still remembered what he said when he gave it to her.

'Life is a gamble,' he had told her. 'Sometimes you win, sometimes you lose. But never give up, and enjoy the ride. Remember that, Caitlyn.'

She took a few deep breaths to calm her emotions. She still had her memories. And she was sure that Sophia was right—it would show up. She rose to her feet and looked in the mirror, dabbing at her eyes. She looked slightly frazzled, but nothing a smile wouldn't fix. It seemed like Sophia was gone for ages, and the minute hand on the clock was creeping closer to the time when she should be walking down the aisle. She poked her head out the door of the bridal room. There was no one around. She figured everyone was already waiting in the hall. She laughed at the thought that she might be late to her own wedding because she couldn't find her maid of honour.

Caitlyn walked to the end of the hallway—there were still people arriving, so they had a little while longer. She peeked around the corner to see an almost full hall, and Andy's best man standing on the stage with the priest, but no Andy. She figured Sophia must still be talking to him. Maybe he was searching his own bag for the token. She decided to go back to the bridal room and wait for Sophia, but stopped in her tracks when she heard voices talking inside a room with the door ajar. She leaned closer to the door, about to open it when she heard Andy's voice, then stopping when she heard Sophia's.

'I'm pregnant.'

There was silence. Caitlyn's breath caught. Sophia was pregnant? But why would she be telling Andy?

'Do you understand what I'm saying?' Sophia asked.

When Andy spoke, his tone was flat, hesitant. And scared? 'Whose?'

'Yours, you idiot,' Sophia said. 'You're the only one I've been with.'

'Oh, God,' he said.

Oh, God. Caitlyn struggled to breathe. How long had she been holding her breath to have the wind knocked out of her? Sophia was pregnant. With Andy's child. He'd cheated on her—with her best friend. She could feel her body shaking, but there were no tears. Her thoughts were scrambled. Should she confront them? Let it go and live with it for the rest of her life? Run? She jumped out of her skin when the wedding planner started talking.

'Caitlyn!' she said. 'What are you doing? You should be in your room! People are still arriving— they'll see you out here.'

Caitlyn closed her eyes for a moment before turning to face her. No doubt Andy and Sophia would have heard the planner talking to her. They would know she was here.

'God, Caitlyn, what's wrong? You look like you've just seen a ghost.'

The wedding planner started fussing over her. Caitlyn turned back towards the room when she heard the door swing open and saw her fiancé and her best friend staring at her like stunned deer in the headlights—or, she should say, *ex*-fiancé and *ex*-best friend. She swallowed, turned away, and ran.

Chapter 4

She stopped running and sat on the park bench, dropping her head onto her hands, her elbows resting on her knees. She let the tears flow. Everything was perfect. Everything had *seemed* perfect. But it had all been a lie. Obviously, Andy had never loved her, and she had been living in a fantasy world all these years. He wanted Sophia—otherwise she wouldn't be pregnant with his child, but Sophia had never let on that she still had feelings for him. However, Sophia had never had any serious relationships since they got together, either. Had they been hooking up the entire time he and Caitlyn were together? How long *had* it been going on for?

She felt numb. How had she not seen it before? Andy and Caitlyn only ever started their relationship and got engaged because of the pressure from their families. Sophia couldn't understand when Caitlyn convinced Andy to hold off on getting married until she'd worked for a few years. Andy was always the wedge between her and Sophia, and she could see that now.

She had nowhere to go. All of her things were at Andy's, since they were already living together. She couldn't go back there. And her family would be so disappointed in her being a runaway bride, and she wouldn't want to ruin their relationship with Andy's parents. Both of their parents had been great friends for as long as she could remember. She wouldn't be able to live with herself if she tore them apart, and she couldn't withhold telling them why she left if she went back to living with them. Sophia was completely out of the question.

Her body shook. What a sight she must look crying on a park bench in a huge white wedding dress.

***

He didn't get much sleep. Axel had spent the whole night worrying how they were going to nail Andy Graeme in court—they still hadn't managed to get any definitive evidence against him, but Cameron had a lead on some possible offshore accounts. Work wasn't really something he wanted to be thinking about while he was trying to relax. Oh, and thinking about Caitlyn. Talk about counterproductive.

He still couldn't get her out of his head, no matter how he tried. He tried reading and couldn't focus. He tried having a long hot shower and wondered what her hair would look like wet. He tried sleeping and, well, that just made things worse. Not even his medication got her out of his head. He knew that he shouldn't be thinking about her at all. He had no right to. She would be getting married today. He knew that shouldn't bother him—he was certain that she never wanted to see him again. And he had thought that he didn't want to see her again. But now, he wasn't so sure. So, he was doing the one thing that he found was most effective when he needed to unwind and get out of his head. He was taking Flop for a run.

He could feel his heart pounding in his chest, his breaths quickening, the endorphins flowing freely and his muscles aching as he ran to the rhythm of the music playing in his ears, Flop running alongside him. And just as he got in the zone and felt as though he was starting to relax, his shoelace came undone. He came to a stop, catching his breath and bent down to tie his shoelace, Flop stretching up to lick his chin.

'I know,' Axel said. 'That feels heaps better, doesn't it, mate?'

Flop responded by licking Axel's chin again.

'Well, we're not quite there yet. Still got a little while to go.'

Axel finished tying his shoelace, took another deep breath and rose to his feet, but Flop was gone.

'Flop!' he yelled, turning until he could see the mischievous terrier bounding towards a woman on a park bench.

Flop was a very affectionate dog and he was not shy. And Axel knew exactly what he does to unsuspecting victims. He called him again, pulling his ear buds out of his ears and racing after him, his heart pounding through his chest when he realised that the woman was wearing a white dress and Flop ran through a puddle to get to her. He pushed harder—he could tell that he wasn't going to make it on time.

'Damn it, Flop!'

He shuddered as Flop took a flying leap onto the woman's lap—muddy paws and all—and started licking her face. The woman shrieked then started laughing from Flop's kisses. He felt his blood drain when he realised that the woman wasn't just wearing a white dress. It was a wedding dress. And it was now getting covered in mud. He finally reached them and grabbed Flop by the collar, but the damage had already been done.

'Flop, get down!' Axel said, lifting the rascal of a dog off the woman's lap. 'I'm so sorry, he got away from me.'

He felt whatever breath he had left leave his body when she looked up at him with the same hyacinth eyes he'd seen two days before and that had kept him awake all night. *Caitlyn*?

'Oh, you have *got* to be kidding me!' he said.

She raised an eyebrow, a hint of a smile pulling on her lips. Wait, she shouldn't be here. He furrowed his brow.

'Aren't you getting married today?' he said. 'Wait, have you been crying?'

'What does it look like, jackass?' she said, squinting.

He took a seat next to her, Flop curling up at his feet. 'It looks like it wasn't a fairy-tale wedding, after all.'

'Do you have to be such a jerk?'

He smiled. 'No, but you seem to bring out the worst in me.'

She frowned, rubbing at a muddy paw print that was drying on her dress. 'Looks like I have a habit of doing that,' she said.

He leaned against the back of the park bench, crossing his arms across his chest. 'Why do I get the feeling that there's a lot more to this story?'

She laughed. 'It might have something to do with me sitting by myself on a park bench in my wedding dress, crying my eyes out,' she said, moving her fingers to tug at a loose thread. 'I stand out like a sore thumb.'

'Well, you're not by yourself now,' he said, nudging her with his elbow. 'And you're not crying anymore.'

A smile crept onto her face. 'I suppose not,' she said. 'Still, it must look strange to see me sitting here in my wedding dress.'

'What happened?'

Did he want her to talk about it? Obviously, the wedding didn't happen. Otherwise she wouldn't be here, in the park, alone, crying. But if her fiancé was the one to end it, he'd imagine that she would be among her friends and family. But here? His guess was that she was a runaway bride. She'd seemed so excited about the wedding two days ago. What changed? And why did he feel as though he wanted to get his hands on the bastard who broke Caitlyn's heart?

***

Did she really feel like talking about it? Of course, she couldn't talk to her family and friends about what happened. Sophia being pregnant with Andy's child would come out soon enough. But maybe talking about it would help her get some closure on the whole ordeal and what better way to gain closure than to talk to a stranger about it? But Axel wasn't a total stranger. But they also hadn't been able to get along with each other in any of their encounters. So, why was he being so nice now? In his totally jerk-like way. She sighed. What did she have to lose? She'd just ran away from everything that she could have lost.

'My maid of honour is pregnant with my fiancé's child.'

His eyes widened. 'I'm not sure I heard that right,' he said. 'Are you saying he cheated on you with your maid of honour? That girl who was at the café with you?'

She nodded.

'And got her pregnant?'

She nodded again.

'And I take it you just found out,' he said, frowning.

'How did you guess?' she said, a smile pulling at her lips.

'Just a hunch,' he said. 'I mean, if you knew before the wedding you probably wouldn't be here in the park in your wedding dress.'

'No shit, Sherlock,' she said, smiling.

'That is, unless you do it just for kicks,' he added. 'But since you were crying, it kind of narrows it down.'

'You just couldn't help yourself, could you?' she said, still smiling.

A cheeky grin spread across his face and his eyes sparkled, making her stomach flip and, before she knew it, she was laughing. Sure, she wasn't laughing hysterically, but she was laughing. And he was making her laugh. She couldn't even remember the last time Andy made her laugh like this. Had he *ever* made her laugh like this?

'So, how did you find out?' he asked. 'Don't tell me they told you right before the ceremony.'

She shrugged. 'I overheard her telling him right before the ceremony. I thought she was going to ask him if he had my *something old*. Obviously not,' she said. She looked down at her hands, clasped together in her lap. 'She was supposed to be my best friend.'

They sat in silence for a few moments, taking in all that was going on around them. The passers-by, the birds singing their songs, the ducks and water birds floating on the lake. The funny thing was, she didn't feel as devastated as she thought she should. Maybe all she needed was a laugh, and Axel brought that to her. She had been foolish, being so blind in her relationship with Andy. But here she was, having a conversation with the man she never thought she would get along with—or see again, for that matter—and enjoying it.

'I'm sorry,' he said, breaking the silence.

She shrugged, still staring at a duck floating past with three ducklings following close behind. 'It's not your fault,' she said.

He turned to face her, uncrossing his arms, sitting on the edge of the seat. 'I meant for acting like a jerk.'

She turned her eyes towards him. His face seemed so sincere, so open. Already, he had her questioning whether she actually had loved Andy, or if it was entirely infatuation with the whole idea of having a perfect life. She supposed perfection was, in reality, nothing more than a pipe dream.

'I'm sorry I stained your shirt,' she said.

He dropped his eyes to the lap of her dress, her eyes followed to see the mud drying on it. 'I guess that makes us even,' he said.

She laughed again. She didn't want to tell him that the wedding dress had cost a significant amount more than his shirt. Not that it bothered her, anyway, since Andy was the one who paid for the dress. She'd rather tear it to shreds and send it back to him than to hang on to it and keep it as clean as she could.

'Did your shirt make it out alive?' she asked, reaching down to give Flop a scratch.

'It probably would have been okay if my sister hadn't used bleach on it,' he said, his lips turned into a side-grin.

She felt her heart skip a beat and warmth spreading to her cheeks. She couldn't remember a simple smile ever creating that kind of emotion for her.

'On a blue shirt?' She surprised herself that she had remembered the colour.

He nodded. 'I guess it's safe to say that it truly is ruined now,' he said, leaning a little closer, their shoulders bumping. 'But now it's her fault, not yours.'

The warmth spread further, and she busied herself by scratching Flop a little more. She lifted the terrier up onto her lap and he curled up, enjoying the attention.

'So, what's your plan now?' Axel leaned back on the bench.

'Working out where to go from here, I suppose,' she said, tugging at a burr that was tangled in Flop's hair. 'All my stuff is at his place.' Because it was never really her home, even though she had been living there for years. 'And I'm not ready to go back to my parents' place. They'd be so disappointed in me for running off from my wedding.'

He raised an eyebrow. 'Disappointed in you? He's the bastard who knocked up your supposed best friend!' Her eyes widened. 'Sorry,' he added. 'But he is. He led you on and played a cruel game. I would never do that.'

***

I would never do that?

His thoughts finally caught up with his mouth. Had he just compared himself to her bastard of an ex-fiancé? What the hell made him do that? She was looking up at him, studying his face, her eyes a deep violet now. And it made him want to lift her chin slightly and press his lips against hers. But he held back. It was, after all, her wedding day. And she had a history of driving him insane. Judging by her reaction earlier when Flop found her on the bench, he probably drove her insane. And, even though they had finally managed to get along so far in this conversation, kissing her would be a big mistake. He didn't want to be the rebound. And he was trekking dangerously close to being it.

He cleared his throat. 'To my fiancée,' he continued. 'If I had one.'

Was he making it worse? Her lips twitched, a smile forming. He looked away, focussing on ...

anything—anything other than her. It was her eyes scrambling his thoughts, it had to be. He'd never seen eyes so beautiful before. He desperately tried to gather his thoughts and tried to ignore the niggling that told him she was single now. The timing was completely wrong. So wrong that it was the wrongest of wrongs. Is that the right word—wrongest? God, he couldn't even think logically. If he could just avoid looking at her …

'Well, I guess I was wrong about you,' she said, her voice a little over a whisper.

Damn it. His head snapped up and he found himself looking into those eyes again. He could feel his resolve slipping away—very quickly.

'Maybe you're not so much of an idiot, after all,' she continued.

He could feel his body stirring, his subconscious was screaming at him to get it together. This woman was dangerous to him—things could go very, very wrong.

'Why don't you come back to my place and get out of that dress?'

Too bad his mouth was an ignorant heat-seeking bastard. He imagined his subconscious facepalming itself. She raised her eyebrows and laughed.

'You don't mess around, do you?' she said, her smile wide and her eyes dancing. She nudged against his shoulder, knocking out whatever reasoning was left in him. 'What makes you think I'd go back with you?'

He shrugged, unable to resist a smile of his own. 'Because you have nowhere else to go.'

She squinted, still smiling. 'But I don't even know you.'

'You know me better than this guy,' he said, indicating to the next person walking past.

'Lounging on the job, are you?' the elderly man said as he walked past.

'Aww, come on! You're finally beating me?' he called after him. Caitlyn raised her eyebrow again at Axel, her body shaking with laughter. 'What, him?' Axel teased. 'The only thing he knows is that I run in this park at the same time every Saturday. He doesn't know me from a bar of soap.'

'And how do I know you won't try to take advantage of me?' she teased, fluttering her eyelashes.

His subconscious started banging its head against its fictitious desk, giving up on telling him just *how* dangerous this woman could be for him. 'Because I'm not that kind of guy,' he said, then shrugged. 'And I live with my sister, so she'll always be around. You'll probably get along with her—you both seem to like mocking me. No doubt she'll let you borrow some clothes, too.'

***

Call her crazy, but the idea was very appealing to her. She didn't want to be around her so-called friends and her family at the moment. And she *certainly* had nowhere else to go. Maybe a change of pace and scenery would be just what she needed. She scratched underneath Flop's chin.

'What do you think, Flop?' she asked. Flop jerked his head up and licked her nose. 'Well, okay, then.' She giggled as the dog tickled her face.

Chapter 5

'Well, this is us,' Axel said, unlocking the front door. He paused before opening it and looked at Caitlyn. 'Umm, my sister has a lot of crazy antics, so just giving you a heads up.'

She nodded. He opened the door, Flop racing in in front of them. It had to be a crazy idea, bringing her back here. Why couldn't his brain win the fight between his brain and his body? Tash was going to give him all kinds of hell for this. He heard Tash shriek from the kitchen and start gushing over Flop. He motioned for Caitlyn to go in first and followed after her, closing the door behind them.

'Dude, how did your run go? You were gone for ages,' Tash said, coming into view, a cup in hand. She stopped mid-step, her expression questioning, and pointed back and forth between Caitlyn and Axel. 'Well, this is new.'

He walked over to Tash as casually as he could and looked back at Caitlyn who was still standing awkwardly near the door. Tash was still staring at her. He cleared his throat.

'Caitlyn, Tash. Tash, Caitlyn.'

Caitlyn smiled. 'Nice to meet you, Tash,' she said.

Tash was still staring, dumbfounded. 'Uhuh,' she said slowly, then pointed to Caitlyn. 'Is that a wedding dress?'

'It is,' Caitlyn said, nodding.

Tash smiled sweetly at Caitlyn, then at Axel. 'Can I talk to you?'

Axel raised an eyebrow, leaning his head over her cup to see what it was. 'Did you just make this?' he asked. Tash nodded, squinting at him. He looked over at Caitlyn. 'Do you want some coffee?'

'I'd love some,' Caitlyn said, relaxing a little.

He pried the cup from Tash's reluctant hand and handed it to Caitlyn, surprising both of them. 'Make yourself at home,' he said. 'We'll be back in a minute.'

He walked through to the kitchen. Tash, following behind him, grabbed two more cups, and started making coffee for himself and Tash. She whacked him on the arm.

'Caitlyn?' she said, almost a whisper. '*The* Caitlyn?'

He nodded. He knew she would freak when she found out.

'What's she doing here?' she continued. 'I thought she hates your guts.'

'Obviously doesn't hate me that much,' he said, smiling at her.

'What's she doing here?'

Axel shrugged. 'She needed somewhere to stay.'

'She's in a wedding dress.'

'You're very observant, sis,' he said, enjoying himself.

She whacked his arm again, then brought her hands to her mouth. 'She was getting married today!' she said. He raised an eyebrow. 'Did you ruin her wedding, expressing your undying love for her?'

He snapped his head towards her. 'What the hell makes you think I would do anything like that?'

'Maybe because there's a *woman* in a *wedding dress* in our *lounge room*,' Tash said through gritted teeth. Axel guessed she really wanted to yell at him. 'And drinking *my* coffee—a girl who you have had a few chance encounters with and haven't managed to get along with at either of them.'

'Flop found her crying in the park,' he explained. 'So, no, I didn't ruin the wedding. It was already ruined. And like I said, she needed somewhere to stay, so I said she could stay here.'

'Stay here?' Tash asked, her voice rising and eyes widening. She lowered her voice again. 'If you guys fight as much as you've led me on to believe, I'm not sure I want her staying here.'

He shrugged. 'We've sort of called a truce.'

'Axel, this isn't a good idea,' she whispered. 'And you know it.'

'She needed help,' he said. 'She has nowhere else to go. And she needs clothes.'

'And you want me to loan her some of mine,' she said flatly.

'Now you're getting it!' he teased, patting her on the head until she grabbed his wrist to stop him.

'Fine, I'll help her, and I'll be nice,' Tash said. 'But I still don't think it's a good idea. It's not going to help with your stress at all.'

'Let me deal with my stress,' he said. 'And you just play a nice hostess.'

He knew that Tash had a point. Having Caitlyn stay here would probably send his stress through the roof. But on the other hand, if they could get along, having some extra company might also reduce his stress. He would still have to deal with it, though. And he would have to make sure he could keep his control and not lose his resolve like he almost did in the park. If—and that's a big *if*—they eventually did end up getting romantically involved somehow, he did not want it to be as a rebound. Rebounds seldom work out, and he knew she had the capability to break his heart.

***

Caitlyn sat on the couch, taking a sip from the much-needed coffee. She felt bad that Axel took it from Tash, but she was also relieved to be able to partake in it so quickly. Besides, she felt a bit better when it sounded like Axel was making more coffee. She could hear them talking in the kitchen, though she couldn't make out what they were saying. But she had a feeling she knew what the topic of conversation was.

Why did she agree to stay with Axel? They hadn't seemed to get along in any of their encounters before that day. But the way he made her smile and the way they seemed to be getting along at the park made her think that it would all be okay. She should know by now that nothing is really perfect. It was only a recent lesson learned—very recent. But when he said that he lives with his sister, she figured it would be okay, not being the only woman in the house. The thought that his sister might not be so happy about it didn't cross her mind.

'How's the coffee?' Axel asked, coming into the lounge room, Tash following behind him. 'I don't think Tash added anything extra to it.'

She smiled. 'It's good,' she said. 'I was thinking, maybe it's not the best idea that I stay here. It's not really fair on you guys to have to put up with me.'

Axel shook his head. 'It's no hassle, right, Tash?' He nudged Tash, who seemed to snap out of her thousand-yard stare.

'Hmm? Oh, no, of course not,' she said, putting her coffee on the coffee table. 'It's fine. Now, let's get you out of that dress and into something more comfortable.'

Caitlyn followed Tash into her room and watched as she rummaged through her cupboard and pulled out some jeans and a shirt. She was very grateful for their help, but she still felt like she was intruding, regardless of what they say.

'You can wear these for now,' Tash said, handing her the clothes. 'Let me know if you need anything else.' She started to leave.

'Umm, Tash.'

Tash paused, her hand on the doorknob, and turned to face Caitlyn. 'Yes?'

'Can you help me?' Caitlyn looked down at herself. 'With the dress?'

'Oh, of course,' Tash said. 'Sorry, I'm not used to having someone in a wedding dress here.'

She walked behind Caitlyn and started working on the tiny pearl buttons running down her back, making quicker work of it than they took to do up.

'It's not fine, is it?' Caitlyn asked.

'The buttons? They're being uncooperative, but I don't mind helping,' Tash said.

'I meant me staying,' Caitlyn said. 'I don't want to put you or Axel out by being here.'

'Oh, don't worry about us,' Tash said. 'Axel is at work most of the time and I could use the company since Liam is having some space at the moment. There!'

She helped Caitlyn step out of the dress and carried it to her wardrobe, hanging it on a coat hanger. Caitlyn pulled on her borrowed clothes.

'Is Liam your boyfriend?'

'Umm, yes, sort of ... well ... kind of.' Tash smiled but Caitlyn wasn't convinced by that, or her mutterings. 'It's complicated. Axel says we have an on-again off-again relationship. So, I guess you could say we're off at the moment.'

'Does that bother you?' Caitlyn asked.

Tash sat on the edge of her bed. 'Not really,' she said, shrugging. 'I mean, I guess it did at first, but we don't see other people in that time. Our breaks are usually so he can concentrate on his work projects, so I suppose we never really break up.'

'I mean, if that's how you guys work. It sucks finding out that your fiancé has been cheating on you with your best friend,' Caitlyn said, staring at the floor.

'Hey, I'm sorry about that,' Tash said. 'It is a rather cruel thing to do. And it is totally fine that you stay here. God, stay as long as you need. I was just worried about Axel, that's all.'

'Why would you worry about him?' Caitlyn asked.

Tash shrugged. 'I just hope he's not putting too much on his plate,' she said. 'I mean, he's already stressed with work. He won't talk about it, but I know it's a pretty big case. And he's been on this medication for it—which you would know about since you filled it for him.'

'Wait, you know about that?' Caitlyn asked, wide-eyed. Had Axel been talking about her to Tash? She wondered what he would have said and the nature of the conversation.

'He may have mentioned it,' Task said. 'But I mean, him being a Good Samaritan, oh, and a guy, he wouldn't have been able to resist helping a beautiful damsel in distress.' She indicated to Caitlyn as she said that, a smile on her face. 'I just hope he doesn't take on too much and end up spiralling.'

'Does he do this a lot?' Caitlyn asked, nervous of the answer. 'Bringing a strange woman home?'

Tash laughed. 'No,' she said. 'This is a first. But I have to admit, I never once imagined he would be bringing a runaway bride home with him.'

Caitlyn grinned. She had to admit, she'd never imagined being a runaway bride. Or staying at someone's place who she'd only just met, for that matter.

*****

They ordered pizza for tea. It seemed to take a little bit of convincing for Caitlyn to agree, but Tash managed to convince her to have some. Sure, it may have been at her expense by laughing at her announcement of a low-carb, low-sugar diet and telling her that she didn't have to make sure she fits in her wedding dress anymore, but she took it lightly. And that made Axel happy. He hadn't been too sure how she would react to Tash's antics and upfront mannerisms, but she seemed to be taking it relatively well.

They ate the pizza in the lounge room, the girls sitting on the couch and Axel sitting on the single armchair to make sure she couldn't sit next to him. If she did sit next to him, he wouldn't be able to resist putting his arm around her—he almost couldn't resist at the park. But she was still very much in the rebound time, even though it was hard to tell since she wasn't acting like she hadn't just run away from her own wedding.

She was laughing, and she had been talking with Tash about nail polish for the last hour, which Tash was ecstatic about since she painted peoples' nails for a living. Well, that's what he thought she did, but she's convinced that her job is as a nail technician—whatever that is. He just didn't get girls. And he especially didn't understand how they could talk colours, and techniques, and different paints for nails for so long. You just pick a colour and slap it on, right? What's so hard about that?

So, he just relaxed in the armchair, ignoring their conversation, and watching the news. Sport, weather, nothing really interesting until a picture of Andy Graeme appeared on the screen, standing in a suit in front of a church. He sat up straighter, on the edge of his seat, his elbows on his knees and turned the volume up.

'Hey, guys, look at this,' he said, waving his hand at the girls.

'Goulburn Candidate for Council and town favourite for Mayor, Andy Graeme, was left at the altar by his fiancée this morning just minutes before the ceremony,' the news presenter said. 'We asked Mr Graeme what went wrong.'

The video flicked to Andy Graeme talking out front of the church. 'It's devastating being left at the altar,' he said. 'There was nothing to indicate that she had ever had cold feet except for watching her hightailing out of there. It's something that can happen to anyone, but I wouldn't even wish it on my worst enemy.'

The video of Andy stopped, and the screen switched back to the presenter in the newsroom. 'Mr Graeme is hoping to be elected for Council and become Mayor in next week's election. Although it's sad that he was left at the altar, it makes us wonder. Was it really a case of cold feet, or does his runaway bride know something we don't?'

Axel turned the volume down as the presenter started talking about other current affairs. He couldn't wait to hear what Cameron thought about that—like he said, their client wanted to see Andy Graeme fall, and Andy Graeme wanted to keep any suspicion out of the public eye. He could see that, regardless of what they uncovered in the court case, the public would already be starting to doubt him. Sure, being left at the altar was a pretty sad thing to have happen, and he did feel bad for him, sort of. But he also knew that this made his case easier. The smile fell from his face when he turned to look at the girls and saw Caitlyn's face pale, then redden.

'Caitlyn?' he asked. 'Are you okay?'

She swallowed, her jaw tense, and pointed at the screen. 'Did you see that?' she said. He had a feeling her question was rhetorical. 'Did you guys see that … that … bastard playing the victim? The victim! *Oh, I got left at the altar by my fiancée and I don't know why*, boo-freaking-hoo!'

Axel's eyes widened. He looked over at Tash whose mouth had dropped open, and back at Caitlyn. He could see the flame in her eyes—but it wasn't the same flame that she had with him at the café and the chemist. This was different. This was fury at its finest. She. Was. Pissed. And there was no stopping her.

'And cold feet?' she continued without pausing for any longer than to catch a breath. 'Seriously? Finding out that the arrogant, good-for-nothing, low-life reprobate cheated on you and knocked up your best friend is not *cold feet*!' She yelled the last two words and jumped to her feet. 'And then he has the … the *nerve* to play the victim all to help his election? Well, screw you, Andy! Screw. You!'

She stalked off to Tash's room and closed the door—hard—behind her. Axel stared at the closed door for a moment before turning to Tash, whose mouth and eyes were still wide open.

'What the hell just happened?' he asked her.

'You brought a psycho home,' she said, shaking her finger at him. 'And now she's in my room and I am officially terrified to sleep tonight.'

He pointed towards the door. There was only one way to explain her reaction, and he wasn't sure if it was a good or bad thing that he had this information in his hands. He wasn't even sure if it was something that he could tell Cameron. He should tell him, of course. It would help them build their case. She might know something and could testify against him, which she might be willing to do since she's clearly so mad at him. It's what Cameron would want to do. But could he do that to Caitlyn? And where would that leave them? He was happy to wait until she was out of the rebound time to test the waters with her, but they didn't have that kind of time before the election and they needed something to cause reasonable doubt on Andy Graeme.

'This woman,' he said, 'was Andy Graeme's fiancée.'

'And you like her,' Tash finished for him. He didn't deny it, though he didn't admit it, either.

'I can't tell Cameron that I know what really happened,' he said.

'No,' Tash said. 'You can't.'

Chapter 6

Axel never thought that he would be back to having sleepless nights. But since meeting Caitlyn, the sleepless nights just slipped back into his life as though they had never left. But now, the thoughts weren't just about the woman in the café or in the chemist who was the pure definition of fury. Now, they were focussed on that woman sleeping in the room next to his, who had just left her fiancé at the altar—Andy Graeme, the very man that he was working on a case against.

Even if she was mad at Andy, he was sure that she wouldn't be happy about him being one of the people working towards bringing him down. But how was he to know that she was Andy Graeme's fiancée until now? Heck, he didn't even know that little piece

                    R.J. Groves

of information when Flop found her in the park. It wasn't until they watched the news the night before. He hadn't seen her after that. According to Tash, she was fast asleep on the mattress they put on the floor for her in Tash's room.

He pulled his shoes on, reading the text message that he just got from Cameron again.

Did you see the news last night? Meet me at the office in two hours.

He knew that, if he was going to be going to the office today, he would probably be there for a while, so he needed to do everything that needed to be done before going in. To put a name to it, he had to buy a new shirt to replace the one the girls had ruined. He opened his bedroom door, prepared to sneak out of the house and found himself staring at Caitlyn's bottom sticking up in the air, wearing yoga pants.

'Oh, hey, dude.' Tash was posing in the same position as Caitlyn. 'You should totally try this!'

Axel stretched his hand out towards them questioningly. 'What the hell are you doing?' He wondered if it was some kind of self-inflicted torture, like jogging or the gym but just … static.

'Yoga,' Caitlyn said, her voice calm. 'Maybe you should try it—it would help with your stress.'

'Guess what this one is called?' Tash said. 'Downward dog! Isn't that hilarious?'

'You look stupid, Tash,' Axel said, laughing.

'I am finding my Zen,' she said, laughing back.

'It might look stupid to you, Axel,' Caitlyn pulled herself up into a standing stretch, 'but it really does help with stress.'

He watched as Tash awkwardly tried to copy what Caitlyn was doing. 'Yeah,' he said. 'I'm not doing that. Anyway, I'm off to buy a new shirt since you two joined forces to destroy my last one.'

'Oh, give me five minutes and I'll come, too,' Caitlyn said.

'No, that's okay,' he said, maybe too quickly. He felt like he couldn't really spend time around her before talking with Cameron and sussing out the situation. 'I have to head over to the office for a while. Cameron has a lead on'—he paused, realising he may have already said too much—'that case we're dealing with. I don't want to keep him waiting. But Tash, can I talk to you for a sec?'

He left quickly, only catching a glimpse of Caitlyn's expression as Tash followed him out the door. Did she look cut? Disappointed? God, he wanted her to come to the shops with him, but after Andy's little performance on the news last night, every man and his dog would be keeping an eye out for the runaway bride. She couldn't be seen in public—not yet, and certainly not with him.

'What's up?' Tash whispered.

'I really do have to go to the office,' he said quickly. 'But I need you to do me a favour.'

'That depends on what it is.'

'I need you to keep Caitlyn inside. Don't let her leave the house, understand?' Tash raised an eyebrow. 'Tash, promise me. She cannot be seen by anyone, not with Andy Graeme and his runaway bride being all over the news.'

'All right, fine.' She pushed him on the shoulder. 'But you owe me one. And don't be too late. Liam's due to be making up with me soon.'

***

She'd scared him off. That's the only reason she could think of for why he ran off so quickly. He didn't even stop to have breakfast, and she was sure that he would have just snuck out of the house without telling her and Tash if they hadn't already been up doing yoga.

She thought of the night before. She thought that she was over it. She knew that she couldn't expect the hurt to just go away so soon after hearing that Andy cheated on her, but she'd thought that she was over him. And she was—over him, that is. Over all of his bull, over his excuses, and overall, over him. She guessed she just needed something big like this to make her realise that she'd been over him for a while and had only been convincing herself that it was still the life she wanted to live. It's as though something clicked inside her and she knew. It still hurt though.

But hanging out with Axel and Tash, despite being off to a rough start with him, had made her feel truly human—not having to please anyone else, not having the pressure to act or talk a certain way, not having to count calories and stick to a diet. She'd enjoyed herself. But it still didn't take away the fact that she'd been led on and betrayed in a really big way, and that was what hurt the most.

And she would have forgotten him. She would have put him to the back of her mind and forgotten about him. But then, he played the victim on the news for all the public to see, making Caitlyn look like the bad guy. Sure, he didn't say her name on the television, but she'd been seen in public with him before, and everyone in this damn town knew that they were together. And she could never forgive him for that. She may have delayed marrying him so that she could get her own degree and work for a little, but he'd hurt her, and he made his decision when he slept with Sophia.

In the past, if she was so angry with someone that she'd cut them out of her life, she would forget them, and the anger would go away. She might be polite to them in a social situation, but she would never go out of her way to talk to them. That's what she intended to do with Andy. But seeing him on the news showed her just how angry she was with him, and made her doubt whether she would even be able to be nice to him in a social situation. She figured that she would never be able to see him, talk to him, or even think about him without her blood boiling.

She was ashamed of how she reacted after seeing Andy on the news. She'd yelled, and called him names, and chucked an all-out hissy fit. She'd never lost it like that before over anyone or anything. Sure, he was completely deserving of it, but she'd cracked it in front of Tash—in front of Axel. That's why she went to bed. She felt like she couldn't look Axel in the eye. She was sure that he would have understood, though he may have been surprised to find out that her ex-fiancé would potentially soon be the Mayor of Goulburn. But him and Tash had stayed silent and she could have cut through the tension with a knife.

She could hear them mumbling in the lounge room after going to bed, but she couldn't make out what they were saying. She'd pretended to be asleep when she heard Tash coming to check on her and heard her tell Axel that she was asleep, even though she whispered to her that she knew she wasn't when she'd closed the door.

She spilled it all to Tash, whispering so that Axel couldn't hear them—how he cheated, Sophia being pregnant, how she found out. All of it. And Tash listened to every word, telling her that he deserved everything she yelled at him through the television. And she'd assured Caitlyn that Axel wasn't freaked out by how she reacted, he was just surprised to find out *who* she was marrying. She'd believed Tash, but seeing Axel rush off to buy a new shirt by himself and supposedly going to the office made her think otherwise.

For starters, why would he need to go to the office on a Sunday? What was so important that it couldn't wait until tomorrow? And the other thing— why wouldn't he want her to go to the shop with him? He couldn't have refused any quicker. Even if he *did* have to go to the office, there would surely be enough time for her and even Tash to go with him to the shops. She was sure that her and Tash could have stayed there longer and found their way back home. Besides, she'd have to buy things soon enough since she had nothing with her except for borrowed clothes from Tash. Maybe she would see if Tash wanted to go with her.

Tash was back inside only a few moments after going out the door with Axel, her expression somewhat changed from her carefree attitude she had while they were doing yoga.

'Everything okay?' she asked.

'Hmm?' Tash said. 'Yep, everything's fine. Hey, I've got this puzzle I've been dying to work on. You should totally help me with it.'

'A puzzle?' Caitlyn said, wondering when the last time she did a puzzle was. 'Okay, sure. But I was thinking that maybe we should go to the shops anyway. I need to get some clothes and I'm not quite ready to go back to Andy's and pick my stuff up.'

Tash's face dropped. 'I don't mind you borrowing mine,' she said. 'Seriously, wear what you want. But I don't feel like going to the shops today and, to be honest, you probably shouldn't be out today anyway. Besides, nothing good is open on a Sunday.'

Tash went to a cupboard, pulled out an unopened puzzle and brought it over to the coffee table, taking a seat on the floor. She looked up at Caitlyn, indicating that she should sit down. She didn't really feel like going out today, but sitting inside not doing much and not being able to be distracted from her thoughts wasn't sounding too appealing to her, either. But Tash saying that she shouldn't go out today confused her.

'Tash, why shouldn't I be out today?' she asked.

'What?'

'You said I shouldn't be out today,' she repeated. 'Why is that?'

'Did I say that?' Tash asked, busying herself with emptying the puzzle pieces from the plastic packets into the box. 'I mean, you *did* just go through the whole Andy thing, like, yesterday. God, if that happened to me, I probably wouldn't be out of the house for weeks.'

'But I'm not like you, Tash,' Caitlyn said, regretting saying it like that when Tash looked cut. 'I can't just sit around and do nothing. I have to get out and do something, that's how I deal with things—by keeping busy.'

'Well, I'm not doing nothing,' Tash said, sorting the pieces. 'I'm doing a puzzle. You can join me, or you can do what you want. That's completely up to you. If you want to go to the shops, I can't stop you. But going out into the public where everyone knows who you are and knows that you ditched your fiancé at your wedding doesn't sound very relaxing to me. Sounds more like putting yourself in front of the firing squad. Not to mention you don't have anything here—not even your purse.'

Caitlyn's mouth dropped open. Tash had a point. She'd been on the news. She'd been seen in public with Andy. Everyone knew her face and associated it with Andy. And now, everyone knows her as his runaway bride. And she'd forgotten that she hadn't gone back to her room at the church to grab her things. She had nothing—no money, no clothes, nothing. She was completely cut off from her world. She closed her mouth.

'I didn't *ditch* him, Tash,' she said, her voice shaking. 'He cheated on me.'

'Oh, I know that,' Tash said, not looking up from the puzzle pieces. 'But the public eye doesn't.'

And it was a point that Caitlyn hadn't thought of before. She knew that Andy cheated on her. Andy and Sophia knew because they're the ones that did it. Axel and Tash only knew because she'd told them. The rest of Goulburn probably thought that she was just a horrible person because she'd left Andy— perfect, sophisticated Andy—at the altar without any warning.

Oh, God, she would never be able to show herself in public again. She would forever be hiding in Axel and Tash's house, wearing Tash's clothes, and never seeing the sun. Maybe it was a slight exaggeration, but that's what it seemed like would happen. She sat down next to Tash and grabbed a handful of puzzle pieces to sort through, resigning to the fact she would have to stay put until it all blew over.

She may as well get comfortable and try to keep herself busy.

Chapter 7

'Caitlyn Low.'

'What?'

'Andy Graeme's fiancée is Caitlyn Low,' Cameron said.

'How do you know her name?' Axel asked, his mind racing. Cameron was already ahead of the game—it wouldn't be long before he finds her.

'Everyone knows her name,' Cameron said. 'She's almost as public a figure as Andy Graeme is, which makes sense since they've been together for years.'

Axel ran his hand through his hair. 'All right,' he said, 'so, how does that help us?'

'It means we know who to look for.'

Look for Caitlyn? What was Cameron's plan? 'I don't see how she can help us,' Axel said, feeling his heart race.

'How could she not help us?' Cameron said, taking a sip of his coffee. 'She ditched him at the altar.'

'I'm sure ditched isn't the right word for it,' he said, realising that he'd just accidentally defended her. Cameron was a savvy man—he was sure that all it would take is a small slip up with the wrong words and he would know that he's hiding something, or rather, someone.

'Oh?' he said, raising an eyebrow. 'What would you call it then? Abandoned? Dissed?'

'What I meant is that I'm sure she would have had a reason for leaving him at the altar,' Axel explained. 'A woman doesn't usually get ready for her wedding and run away when she's supposed to be walking down the aisle unless she has a good reason.' Like finding out she was about to marry a cheating bastard.

'Are you an expert on women, now?' Cameron said, stretching his arms out towards Axel. 'Axel Taylor—a man who understands women.'

Axel laughed. At least Cameron seemed to not suspect anything. 'Can any man truly understand women?' Axel said. 'It was just a little bit of insight that Tash let me in on when we saw it on the news.'

'Sure, sure,' Cameron said. 'Well, that is right—she would have a reason, right? So, we need to find out what that reason was. Did she find out he's been up to some shady business? Had he been blackmailing her? Is she pregnant? If we find her and find out the reason, she could testify against him.'

Is Caitlyn pregnant? Well, that's not the story that he heard, but he couldn't tell Cameron what he did know because he couldn't subject her to having to testify against Andy Graeme. He saw how she reacted by simply seeing him on the news. Seeing him face-to-face in court could end up getting her arrested for assault. He shook his head.

'Wait, why would she leave him if she found out she was pregnant?' he asked. 'That's a normal progression after marriage. Wouldn't it be more of a reason for her to leave if she found out he'd gotten someone else pregnant?'

Cameron raised his eyebrow at Axel. 'Do you know something that I don't, Axel?'

Axel felt the cells in his body racing. 'I'm just trying to think of a logical reason why she would leave,' he explained. 'It doesn't seem logical to me for her to leave if she was pregnant. But if, for example, she'd just found out that he'd gotten someone else pregnant, that would make her run for sure.' He hoped that he had said it in a way that made it sound as though he was just thinking of possibilities instead of that he knew something.

'You haven't met our client yet, have you?' Cameron asked, his expression somewhat solemn. 'And I'm pretty sure you don't know why he's after Andy Graeme.'

Axel shook his head. He'd always wondered what the details were, but Cameron had only ever told him what he felt he needed to know—that the client wanted to see Andy Graeme brought down.

'Come with me,' Cameron said, leading Axel into one of the conference rooms where a man in his fifties sat. 'Meet Colin Jefferson. Colin, this is Axel Taylor, he's helping me with your case. I think it's time that we fill him in on all the details.'

'I've been telling you that for weeks, Cameron,' Colin said. Axel and Cameron took a seat opposite him.

'The reason why Mr Jefferson wants to see Andy Graeme brought down, Axel,' Cameron started, 'is because he believes that Andy had a hand in the murder of his daughter, Faith, four years ago.'

Axels mouth dropped open. 'Murder?' he said in disbelief, then looked at Colin. 'I'm so—'

'Sorry for my loss?' Colin finished for him. 'I've heard it all before. But you can help me by bringing that bastard down.'

'Okay, but are we sure that he could be capable of that?' Axel asked, still trying to wrap his head around it. 'I mean, he doesn't really strike me as someone who would be capable of murder.'

'Anyone could be capable of murder, Mr Taylor,' Colin said, leaning across the table. 'You would be surprised how many people have killed someone but appear to be a good person in the public eye.'

'The point is,' Cameron said, drawing their attention back to their case. 'Mr Jefferson has reasonable grounds to suspect that Andy Graeme may have been behind it.'

'Which is?' Axel prompted.

'The supposed killer came forward some months back, pleading guilty,' Cameron explained. 'He's in prison now, but it doesn't all add up.'

'Well, if he pleaded guilty, he obviously did it, right?' Axel asked.

'Not necessarily,' Cameron said. 'See, Mr Jefferson and his daughter were very close. So close that she told him everything.'

'She was pregnant,' Colin said, a tear in his eye. 'She said that Andy Graeme was the father. They'd been spending a lot of time together. I'—his voice broke—'I told her to tell him—any guy who is half a gentleman would do the right by her. He told her to get rid of it and she said no. He sent her money a few days later and she sent it back to him. I lost all respect for that man that day.'

Faith was pregnant? So, the bastard had a habit of knocking up unsuspecting girls. Axel felt his body heating up. God, he would love to see this guy brought down.

'Faith was killed in a car accident when she was coming home from work a week after telling him that she was pregnant,' Cameron finished, his tone deep. 'It was ruled as an unfortunate accident until the killer stepped forward.'

'So, where are we at with his finances?' Axel asked. Surely, there must be some way they can get him for it.

'We've found the records of the money he'd sent to her, proof that she'd sent it back, and another transaction of the same amount being sent to the man who pleaded guilty for her death,' Cameron said. 'We're still looking into the rest of his finances.'

'Shouldn't that be enough to get him?' Axel asked.

Cameron shook his head. 'It shows the transactions taking place, the rest is hearsay,' he said. 'We need someone to testify against him to have a real edge on him. So, we need to find Caitlyn Low, find out what she knows—why she ran—and see if she'll testify against him.'

'And if we can't find her?' Axel asked.

'We keep looking,' he said.

'What about the guy in prison?' Axel suggested. 'If Andy Graeme paid him to do that, he could testify.'

'He won't talk,' Cameron said.

'Have you tried?'

'No, but if he was going to talk, he would have brought Andy down with him when he was being trialled.'

'Unless he was being threatened,' Axel said. 'We have to try. We can't put all of our eggs in one basket. If Caitlyn doesn't talk, we need someone who will.'

'I agree,' Colin said. 'See, Cameron? I told you we should have told him weeks ago.'

Cameron sighed, a smile pulling at his lips. 'Fine,' he said. 'I'll set it up.'

* * *

'I'm home,' Axel called from the front door.

'We're in here!' Tash yelled back.

Caitlyn picked up another puzzle piece and moved it along the half-completed puzzle, smiling as it fell into place. She stroked Flop's back, who had settled into her lap. Despite being reluctant to work on the puzzle at first, she'd actually really enjoyed it and it managed to distract her so much that she hadn't realised that it had been hours since Axel left.

'Is that my puzzle?' Axel asked.

Caitlyn startled. How did she not hear him sneaking up behind her? Was she that focussed on the puzzle?

'Aww, it is!' he continued. 'Damn it, Tash, you know I've been holding out to do that.'

'Wait, *your* puzzle?' Caitlyn asked, looking up. 'I thought Tash said it was hers.'

She looked over at Tash, who shrugged. Axel glared at Tash.

'Oh, she would have,' he said. 'She lays claim to anything I have that's cool.'

'You can still help us with it,' Tash said. 'We just made a start on it.'

He looked it over. 'Sure,' he said, taking a seat on the couch behind her. 'Just save the last piece for me.'

He turned the television on and started flicking through the channels, stopping on the news. Caitlyn looked up at the screen when she heard the voice that she'd grown familiar with.

'There'll be a reward for anyone who knows any information on where she might be,' Andy said.

'I just want her to come home,' her mother said between sobs.

Andy put his arm around her mother. 'We all do,' he said into the camera.

The video flicked back to the reporter in the newsroom. 'This concern for Caitlyn Low's safety stems from an anonymous tip saying that a woman matching her description was seen sitting in a park in her wedding dress with a man in workout gear and his dog at the time of the wedding. The man apparently runs in the park every Saturday, though his name is unknown. If you know anything about Caitlyn Low's disappearance, please call the number on the screen.'

The screen went black and Axel tossed the remote onto the couch.

'Damn it!' he yelled, making her jump.

She turned to face him, her chest aching when she saw he had his head resting in his hands.

'Axel,' Tash said, quietly.

'That man!' he hissed, startling her again. He looked up at the black screen, his eyes on fire. 'The guy who walked past us.'

'The one you spoke to?' Caitlyn asked.

He nodded. 'It had to be him,' he said. 'That's my running spot!'

'Axel,' Tash repeated.

'Now, I won't be able to run there anymore!' Flop looked up at Axel and whined. 'That son of a—'

'Axel!' Tash said again, loudly this time.

'What?'

'They're looking for you,' she said. 'They're looking for both of you.'

'They don't know who I am,' he said.

Tash shook her head. 'It won't take them long,' she said. 'Now that the first tip has been sent in, everyone who saw you guys will be sending theirs.'

They both looked at Caitlyn, his expression dropping to one of concern.

'Caitlyn, are you okay?' he asked.

Was she? She put her hand to her cheek—it was wet. She could feel her body shaking. When had she started crying? She'd never meant to put Axel in this situation—or Tash, for that matter. Axel had offered her a place to go and she took him up on his offer. How was she to know that Andy and her parents would order a search for her and get all of Goulburn looking for her? Now, people would think she'd been kidnapped. And that would be bad for Axel. God, what a mess she'd made!

'I'm so sorry,' she stammered. 'This is all my fault, I didn't mean for this to happen.'

'Honey, it's not your fault,' Tash said. 'It's that sorry excuse of a man. He's the one who cheated on you.'

'But I didn't think,' she said, taking a breath in an attempt to stop her voice from shaking. 'I didn't think that they would think I'm missing and put it all over the news.' She looked down at her hands, picking at her nails. 'I didn't think they would care.'

'It's your family, Caitlyn,' Axel said, sliding onto the floor next to her. He pulled her into his arms. 'Of course they would care.'

'He gave up the right to care about me when he slept with Sophia,' she sobbed into his chest.

She could feel his strong arms around her and it was soothing. He was rubbing her back with his hand—his touch was like electricity pulsing through her body. And the woody aroma of his cologne warmed her and made her hungry. But hungry for food or hungry for him, she wasn't sure. She pressed herself further against him and he rested his chin against her head. He was comforting. He made her feel safe. She had never felt like that with Andy.

'Caitlyn, you need to tell your mother you're okay,' Tash said.

'Tash is right,' Axel said, pulling her back to look at her face. 'You have to tell her you're okay so that she can call off the search for you.'

And not search for him as a kidnapper—she was sure that was what he was thinking. Talk to her mother? Sure, she might have acted devastated on the television, but she wouldn't understand the reason why she left in the first place. Her mother had always been set on her marrying Andy. And, as much as she didn't want to talk to her, she had to. For Axel and Tash's sakes. She couldn't let the situation escalate any more than it already had.

'You're right,' she said, wiping her tears with the back of her hand, and missing having Axel's arms around her, even though she shouldn't. 'I don't want to talk to her, but I will. I have to.'

'Good,' Axel said, brushing a stray hair behind her ear, his thumb lingering against her cheek. 'But you can't tell her where you're staying.'

'Oh, don't worry,' Caitlyn said. 'I wouldn't dream of it.'

He smiled at her and it warmed her from the inside out. God, he had a gorgeous smile. She hadn't noticed until now. She could get used to seeing it—to seeing him—but she knew that she shouldn't. She was sure that his tender touch was just because of the moment, full of compassion and comfort. And his eyes—so sincere. She could truly get lost in them. She could get lost with him. God, she hoped it wasn't just because of the moment.

Tash cleared her throat, startling her, and Axel dropped his hand from her cheek and was on his feet quicker than she could blink.

Damn.

Chapter 8

'You have to tell her.'

Axel had just finished telling Tash about what Cameron and Colin talked to him about in the office. They both knew that Caitlyn didn't leave Andy at the altar because of what happened with Faith Jefferson, even if that's what Cameron thought. But they also figured she wouldn't have stayed with him for so long if she did know about it.

'I can't,' he whispered.

They tried to keep their voices low while Caitlyn readied herself in Tash's bedroom to go through with their plan. They decided to wait until dark. Caitlyn would dress up so that she looked like Tash leaving the house with Axel, he would drive her to her parent's place, she would sneak in the back with the hidden spare key and talk to her mother. It would be quick, simple, straightforward. Nothing should go wrong. No one else should see them. No one would be any the wiser.

'Axel, this isn't just a fling in the playground we're talking about,' Tash whispered back. 'This guy is being accused of being associated with *murder*.'

'There's no proof yet,' he said. 'The evidence is rocky at its best. It's just a few figures on his financial accounts—it doesn't mean the payments are related.'

'Sounds pretty obvious to me,' Tash said.

'I shouldn't even be telling you this, anyway,' he said back, pulling his black hoodie on. 'How do I look?'

'Like you're about to rob a bank,' she said.

Axel smiled. 'Great.'

'Axel, I don't like the idea of you dealing with him. What if he's there? And it's true? What if he *is* a murderer?'

'Let's not jump to conclusions yet, Tash,' Axel said. 'We need proof first. And Caitlyn says that he has a meeting tonight, so he won't be anywhere in sight.'

'Still,' Tash said. 'You have to tell her.'

He shook his head.

'Tell me what?'

He turned to face Caitlyn. Her brow was furrowed. God, she looked so innocent. She was wearing a pair of Tash's jeans and favourite black hoodie. They'd told her that if she wore those, everyone would mistake her for Tash. Her eyes were a deep violet tonight, with that fire flaring in them that he'd found attractive. Tonight had to go well. It seemed simple enough. They just had to keep going with the plan.

'It's time to go,' Axel said quickly. 'You have to remember not to tell your mother where you are staying.'

'I said that I wouldn't,' she said.

Axel raised an eyebrow. Out of every emotion that he thought she would be feeling right now, he hadn't expected bored to be one of them. He wondered what the nature of her relationship with her mother really was like. Her mother had seemed so devastated on the news. He was starting to get the vibe that maybe she wasn't as close to her mother as he thought.

'But that's not what you have to tell me,' she continued.

Axel glared at Tash, then started walking towards the door, pausing as he got level with Caitlyn.

'I can't tell you what you want to hear,' he said, his voice low. As much as he knew he had to tell her, he also wanted to avoid doing it until there was no other way. He wanted to protect her, and she wouldn't be happy with the news. 'But I'm taking care of it, trust me.'

She squinted up at him. 'I'm having a hard time trusting anyone at the moment,' she said. 'Especially when they're hiding something from me.'

He swallowed. He wouldn't be able to win either way. She would be mad that he'd hidden something from her, and she would be mad when she found out what it is. They were from two different worlds, two different make-ups. The sooner he realised that anything with her could never work, the better. When this all blows over, they could go their separate ways. But he couldn't help feeling that a part of him would go with her.

***

His eyes were cold. His eyes that had looked at her before and filled her with warmth were now cold as steel. It chilled her to the bone. Had she imagined the warmth that was there before? Maybe coming back to his place was a bad idea after all. It was starting to work out to be more complicated than she thought it would. She never wanted to be a hassle for him.

'Let's go,' he said, moving past her towards the door.

She glanced over at Tash, questioning her with her eyes. Tash shrugged.

'Have fun, guys,' Tash said. 'Don't get caught.'

Caitlyn rushed to catch up with Axel who was already out the door, waiting just out the front. She wasn't so sure about their plan now. She was okay with it earlier, when she felt assured by him. But she wasn't sure she could carry this out with him being so cold. What changed?

'Why can't you tell me?' she asked.

'It's not the time,' he said under his breath. 'Just keep your head low and don't stop until you get to the car.'

'Seriously?' He was going to tell her what to do now?

'Just *do* it!'

She was about to tell him to lay off, when she heard a man's voice coming from behind them.

'Tash, wait!'

'Keep walking,' Axel mumbled to her, turning towards the man and waiting for him to catch up. 'She doesn't want to talk to you, Liam. You left it too long.'

She kept walking.

'What?' Liam's voice sounded cut.

'Tash is pissed,' Axel said, then lowered his voice so that not even Caitlyn could hear what he said.

She reached the car, opening the door, and climbing in, not closing the door shut completely in an attempt to hear what they were saying.

'Thanks, man,' Liam said. 'I'll, ahh, wait for her.'

Axel talked louder again. 'I'll try to talk her into hearing you out.'

She closed the door fully as Axel got in next to her and started the car. She reached up to brush her hood down, looking at Axel in surprise when he reached over to stop her hand.

'Leave the hood on,' he said. 'In case someone sees us.' He let her hand go.

She dropped her hand into her lap, feeling the tingle where his hand had touched. 'Was that Tash's boyfriend?'

'Liam?' Axel said. 'I guess you could call him that. They're together, if that's what you mean. Most of the time, anyway.'

She smiled. Tash had told her about her on-again off-again relationship with Liam. She didn't really understand how it worked, but it obviously worked for them.

'What did you say to him?' she asked, looking up at Axel.

He glanced over at her and she could see that his eyes didn't look as cold as they did before. He smiled. 'I told him to go inside. I didn't want to say Tash was really in there in case someone overheard us, but I know he has a key and she can explain everything to him.'

She dropped her gaze. 'Would he tell anyone? He would have seen the news, too, right?'

'You have nothing to worry about with Liam,' he said. 'You can tell him the darkest of secrets and know he wouldn't spill to anyone even if they tried to torture it out of him.'

'Well, I hope it doesn't come to that.' She smiled.

He glanced back at her, his eyes wide. She cleared her throat. Maybe it wasn't good timing for a joke like that.

'Can I get secrets out of you?' she asked, still wondering what him and Tash were talking about before.

'Depends what it is,' he said, a smile forming on his face.

'Is it something that I should know?'

He stayed silent, focussing on the drive. She could feel the coolness coming between them again.

'What you're not telling me, Axel,' she continued, 'is it something that I need to know, or does it not concern me?'

'Yes.'

Yes?

'Axel,' she started.

'Yes, Caitlyn,' he said, startling her with his tone. 'It concerns you. And you do need to know what it is. But I'm not telling you—not yet.'

'Why not?'

'Because I'm not ready to.'

'*You're* not ready to tell me?' she said, furious. 'Since it concerns me, why don't you try telling me when *I'm* ready?'

'Caitlyn,' he said.

'No, seriously, Axel,' she said. 'I'm ready now.'

'Let it go,' he said, his voice more like a growl.

'Why?'

'Because I don't want you freaking out about it until I've got all the facts right.'

'Am I likely to freak out?' she asked, raising her eyebrow.

He shrugged, then nodded. 'Probably.'

'And you're sure you're not ready to tell me?'

'Caitlyn,' he warned.

'Fine,' she said, leaning back against the seat.

They spent the rest of the drive silent except for Caitlyn's directions to her parent's house. She couldn't understand why Axel wouldn't tell her what it was, especially since it concerned her and even more because she would supposedly freak out about it. But at the same time, she respected his decision to keep it quiet until he knew the facts. But what was it? And how would he have come across something that concerns her without her being in on it?

When they got to her parent's place, Caitlyn was relieved to see that her mother's car was the only car in the driveway. At least that would make it easier.

'Are you ready?' Axel asked, pulling the car over to the side of the road.

She took a big breath and nodded slowly. 'I think so,' she said.

'Do you want me to come in with you?'

She looked over at his steel-grey eyes that were warm again. God, how could they change so quickly? She wasn't ready to go in and talk to her mother. She wanted Axel to come in with her. At least he would make sure she went in and actually talked to her without chickening out. But he couldn't. Her mother couldn't know who Axel was. No one could know who she was with because she didn't want Andy finding her. She didn't want to see his cheating face and sure as hell didn't want to talk to him. She would rather go for the rest of her life without even thinking of him again.

Which is why she had to talk to her mother. So that the whole wedding thing can be left in her past and she can move on with her life. She took another breath.

'No,' she said. 'Can't have her seeing you.'

'True,' Axel said, looking out the window of the car towards the house. 'Is she home?'

'Her car is here,' Caitlyn said. 'So, I'd say so.'

'You better be quick, then,' he said, smiling at her. 'Before anyone else comes home.'

'Right,' she said, hesitating with her hand on the car door handle. God, what was she even going to say to her mother? She hadn't really thought this through.

'Do you want me to push you out of the car?'

Caitlyn laughed, glancing at Axel. He had a cheeky grin on his face. She felt her heart flip in her chest. Why did he have to be so damn cute?

'All right,' she said, opening the door. 'I'm going.'

'Have fun!' he said as she closed the door.

Fun wasn't exactly what she would call talking to her mother. She'd never had to explain to her mother why she didn't marry the supposedly perfect man that had been lined up for her before. But there's always a first, right? She walked quickly in the shadows until she got to the back door, found the spare key, and opened the door, stepping inside. Everything was still exactly where it was when she was a child—in its place. She'd navigated this house in the dark many times before, sneaking in late through the back door and hiding the key back outside the next morning. She could hear movement in the lounge room and edged towards it, ramming her shin into the edge of a coffee table.

'Ouch!' She clamped her hand over her mouth, trying to stay quiet while the pain pulsed through her leg.

'Who's there?' her mother called out, her voice shaking a little.

She stopped moving, her heart pounding through her chest. Was it too late to run again? The light flicked on.

'Caitlyn,' her mother said, surprised. 'What are you doing here?'

Chapter 9

'So, you really missed me, huh?' Caitlyn said.

She knew it was all a façade. Nothing much really seemed to be real with her mother. She knew it would be pointless, but Axel had such high hopes that it would work. Maybe she would get Andy to lay off the news. Maybe her mother would make sure that she wasn't actually listed as a missing person.

'Of course I did,' her mother said, stepping closer. Caitlyn took a step back. Her mother's face dropped. 'Why did you run away?'

'He didn't tell you?' she scoffed.

'Tell me what?'

'He cheated on me,' she said.

'So?'

So? That's all she could come up with? Andy—her fiancé—had cheated on her and all her mother could say about it was *so*? Caitlyn couldn't believe it. She hadn't expected her mother to be overly sympathetic, but she thought she might have at least been understanding. Oh, how she'd underestimated her mother's lack of empathy in times when she might need some motherly advice.

'What?'

'You don't run away, Caitlyn,' her mother said. 'You deal with it. You stay, and you deal with it.'

'I'm not sure you understand what I'm saying, Mother,' Caitlyn said.

'You don't think your father never had his affairs since we've been together?' she asked. 'I know what you are saying. And I'm telling you what you do about it.'

'He got her pregnant!'

'You should have married him, Caitlyn. You could have overlooked it and had the security that you won't have now. You have no one to blame but yourself. You should never have put off getting married to him just to go off and mess around getting a degree. What use would it be anyway if you're married and having a family? Well, I suppose you will get use out of it now, since you threw that lifestyle away.'

'I did that degree because I wanted to do something with my life,' she said defensively. 'But I didn't come here to hear your lecture about the choices I've made in my life. I came to tell you to call off the search party. I'm not missing, I haven't been kidnapped. I just didn't want to be found or talk to any of my so-called friends and family.'

'Well, now you've said it,' her mother said. 'You can leave.'

'What?'

'There's nothing else for you to say,' she said, her eyes regarding Caitlyn without flinching. 'You made a decision, so now you have to live with it. Coming back here is not an option.'

Caitlyn swallowed. That was the point she finally realised there was nothing left for her in the life that she was used to living.

***

Axel watched her until she was around the back. She'd blended in well with the shadows—only someone who knew where to look would be able to see her. He sighed, resting his head against the headrest of the car seat. Caitlyn's determination to know what he wasn't telling her made him smile. He hadn't lied—he did want to know all the facts before telling her. But it was more the fact that he had to work out the right way to tell her.

From what he could work out, she would be mad about it either way—not that it should matter, since they wouldn't work out anyway. He really should just treat it like a Band-Aid and rip it off. It would hurt initially, but it would be quick, instead of prolonging the pain. He closed his eyes for a moment. How had he managed to get to a point where he cares about her more than he should?

When this has all blown over, and the election has finished, and the court case has been processed, she would be out of his life. She would go back to her family, and walk among her social group. She may have had nowhere else to go for now, but it wouldn't be too long before she missed her family and her friends, and wanted to go back to them.

In such a short time she'd wound herself tightly into Axel's life, driving him crazy in both his body and his mind. He admired her persistence and determination, but at the same time, it almost drove him to breaking point. Even if she didn't go back to her life, he had to be careful about who he let into his. He didn't need the extra stress. Simply having her around was stressful. He knew that they wouldn't work, and he had to keep telling himself that. But he still couldn't ignore the chemistry that was obviously there between them.

Sure, sometimes it was a sizzle—a warmth, tenderness—when they could get along, but there was also the bang of chemicals that react together when they couldn't. And it's the bang that is the strongest reaction.

He felt more attracted to her every time he saw that flame burning in her eyes.

Every time he sees the sadness in her eyes, he wants to make it go away.

Having her in his arms before, he didn't realise what he was doing until it was too late. He didn't register his body slipping to the ground next to her and pulling her close to him. He saw a woman who needed comforting and he did it without thinking. He didn't think that her pressing closer to him would have hazed his thoughts or even make him forget that Tash was there, too. She was a mess—a beautiful mess. And she was too dangerous for him.

His eyes jerked open when his phone started ringing. He glanced towards the house—no sign of Caitlyn yet. He answered.

'Hi, Cameron.'

'Axel, I need you down at the office,' Cameron said. 'Our finance guy has picked something else up. How soon can you be here?'

'I'm in the middle of something at the moment, Cameron,' he said.

He heard a door slamming and glanced towards the house in time to see Caitlyn storming back towards the car.

'I think the answer you're looking for is *ten minutes*,' Cameron insisted.

'I'll be there as soon as I can,' he said, hanging up the phone as Caitlyn opened the car door and flopped into the seat, pulling her hood back from her head.

'Let's go,' she said, her tone filled with anger.

Axel started the car. 'So, it went well?' he asked.

She glared at him. 'By *well*, do you mean exactly as I thought it would?' she asked, leaning her head against the headrest. 'Then yes, it did. Her lack of empathy didn't surprise me one bit.'

'Is she calling off the search?'

'Who would know?' she said, closing her eyes. 'Going to her was a stupid idea.'

'Caitlyn, what happened?' he asked, glancing over at her. He wished he could have gone in there with her, but he knew that they couldn't risk her mother seeing who she was with, not with all the gossip about her being kidnapped going around.

'She kicked me out,' she said, furrowing her brow, her eyes still closed. 'Told me that it was all my fault anyway and kicked me out.'

'That bastard cheating on you isn't your fault, Caitlyn,' he said. Surely, she didn't believe that?

She shrugged. 'Well, maybe it is,' she said quietly. 'I mean, I *did* go to Melbourne to study my degree instead of staying close by. I just wanted to do something with my life instead of tying myself down.'

'Do you really think marriage is tying yourself down?' Not that it should matter to him.

She smiled, glancing over at him. 'My ideal marriage wouldn't be. But it certainly would have been with him. Hey, Axel?'

'Yes?'

'Can we just drive around for a little bit?' she asked, her eyes pleading. 'I don't feel like I'm ready to go back home yet.'

He would have liked nothing better, but he wasn't sure it would be a good idea. Driving around together meant they would get to know each other better and that would just make it harder for him to let her go when she decided she missed her normal life.

'We can,' he said, hesitating before continuing, 'but I do have to drop past the office.'

'Is that code for something?'

'What?'

'Dropping past the office,' she explained. 'I mean, I know you're a lawyer, but don't you get the weekends off?'

'Sometimes,' he said, responding to her gentle teasing. 'But this is for a very time-sensitive case, so I pretty much have to be on call whenever Cameron hears anything.'

'I take it Cameron is the lawyer you work with?'

He nodded. 'Do you want me to drop you back home? I'm not sure how long I'll be.'

She shook her head. 'No. I can wait in the car. I'm sure you won't be there all night.'

'All right.'

They drove in silence for a few minutes, Caitlyn staring out the window. Axel kept glancing over to take all of her in, and he couldn't work it out, but he kept wondering if something had changed for her when she talked to her mother. Obviously, there was the fact that her mother was totally unsupportive of her decision, but he didn't think that was all there was to it.

'Do you miss your normal life?' he asked, breaking the silence.

'There's nothing for me there,' she said, dropping her gaze to her hands before glancing up at him. 'I don't think there ever was, to be honest. I never liked conforming to all the rules.'

'So, what would your ideal marriage be like?' he asked, surprising himself.

Had he seriously just asked that? He imagined his subconscious banging its head against a desk again. He had to work out how he could control what his mouth says when he's around this woman or he'd end up losing the ability for rational thought. He stopped himself from glancing over at her, focussing on driving the car, but he could feel her eyes on him.

***

Her ideal marriage? Who asks that? She smiled. She could tell that he was trying to avoid looking at her, even while she was looking at him. Had he really meant to ask that? It wasn't something she figured would usually pop up in general conversation. But then, they hadn't exactly had a usual anything since they've met. Most people don't start off with not being able to get along, then ending up staying in the same house, and having the public mistake a runaway bride for a kidnapping all in the space of a few days. It might be quicker to list everything that *was* normal with their interactions.

'Well,' she started. 'I'd want to keep working. For a while at least.'

'That's fair enough.'

She raised an eyebrow at him. 'I'd want it to be a dependently independent relationship.'

He glanced over at her. 'What's that even mean?' he asked.

'It means that I don't want to be so independent of each other that it comes between the relationship,' she explained. 'I would be dependent on him, he would be dependent on me, and together, we would be independent.'

'That's the way it should work anyway, isn't it?' It certainly sounded scarily similar to the way he had always viewed marriage.

'I think so,' she said. 'What about you?''

'What about me?'

'What would your ideal marriage be?' she asked.

'Supportive,' he said, thinking for a moment. 'Both ways, not just her supporting me. And stress-free, preferably.'

She laughed. She didn't mean to, but she did. He pulled over to the side of the road and turned to face her. The smile dropped from her face.

'I'm sorry, Axel,' she said. 'But can a marriage really be stress-free?'

'I can think of ways to make it less stressful,' he said, winking at her.

She felt a blush rising to her cheeks and looked away. She felt bad for laughing. He didn't laugh at any of her points. In fact, he'd agreed with her. And she agreed that a marriage should be supportive both ways, but there would always be stresses in life and some of them were bound to make it into a marriage.

     R.J. Groves

'Did you pull over because I laughed?' Caitlyn asked, risking a glance up at him.

He was smiling.

'No,' he said. 'I pulled over because we're here.'

'Oh,' Caitlyn said.

She watched as he left the car and walked across the road into the office, wondering what could be so important that he had to go to the office twice in one day. Why couldn't it wait until tomorrow morning? It really wasn't that far away. She took her seatbelt off and leaned her head back against the headrest again, closing her eyes. She was relieved to know that Axel took her laughing at the whole stress-free marriage thing lightly. He'd had her fooled, thinking that he pulled over because of it. She hadn't realised that they were out front of the office. In saying that, how could she have known? She knew that he was a lawyer, but at no stage had he mentioned where he worked.

She looked back over at the office, reading the name on the sign. *Landon Legal*. Why did that name sound familiar? She heard a tap on the passenger-side window and jumped when her door flung open.

'You shouldn't have run, Caitlyn.'

Chapter 10

'So, what's so important it couldn't wait until tomorrow?' Axel asked.

'The discrepancies in his finance records,' Cameron said, handing him the sheets with numerous numbers highlighted.

Axel looked at the numbers and shook his head. 'What does this mean, Cameron?'

'See that first number? The one that's green?' Cameron said, pointing to the numbers. Axel nodded. 'That was made nine years ago—one bulk payment and an ongoing monthly payment to an account owned by a woman. The next two are large payments made to the same account owned by a known heavy drug dealer in Sydney who's into some crazy stuff, almost a year apart from each other.

Within a short time after the first payment was made, a woman went missing and was found dead some time later. Same for the second payment—another woman went missing and was found dead. Both were pregnant.'

'What happened to the drug dealer?'

'Charged with multiple counts of murder and serving life in a high-security prison,' Cameron said. 'But there's more. The numbers highlighted in pink are the transactions regarding Faith Jefferson—the money he sent her that she returned, and the same amount being sent to the guy who's serving time for her death.'

Axel pointed to the number. 'That's the same amount the drug dealer got sent for the others.'

Cameron nodded. 'But look at the last one.'

Axel scanned down the page until he hit the last highlighted number that was the same as the others. He looked up at Cameron.

'That one was deposited into an account owned by the guy who killed Faith two years ago, a few months before he came clean.'

'Do we know what it was for?'

Cameron shook his head. 'But I plan on asking him when we go to see him tomorrow.'

'So, what you're saying,' Axel said, putting the pages down on the desk. 'Is that Andy Graeme could be guilty for aiding and abetting in the murder of at least three people?'

'And possibly a fourth.'

Axel ran his hand through his hair. Could what Cameron is saying be true? If it is, their case just escalated to a whole other level, much more than he signed up for. This would be a huge accusation—one that shouldn't be made without solid evidence. But they were running out of time.

'When do we go to the prison?' he asked.

'First thing in the morning,' Cameron said.

Axel's eyes shot up towards the door to the sound of a car horn sounding. It sounded a few times—quick and sharp—then once for longer. He could feel his mind racing. That wasn't someone sounding the horn at someone going past. It was a very distinct, deliberate sound.

'What the hell?' Cameron said, heading towards the window to glance out.

And then a scream.

Axel was on his feet before he could even think of what to do. 'Caitlyn!'

***

'Let me go!'

Caitlyn tried to reach across to sound the horn again, but it was just out of reach. She focussed her efforts on getting out of Andy's grasp instead.

'Just get out of the car!' he yelled, pulling her by the leg until he could reach her arm.

She threw hits at his arm—the one that had hold of her by the wrist—until he let go of his hold, and kicked his knee, managing to push him back far enough to get out of the car and start running towards Axel's office. She didn't get very far before he grabbed her by the arm and pressed her against the side of the car, his arm across her throat. She tried to move her legs, her arms, anything, but he had her pinned.

She felt trapped, helpless, and her neck ached where he had his arm pressing against her. How had it come to this?

'Get *off* me, Andy!' she yelled in his face.

'You shouldn't have left me, Caitlyn,' he snarled. 'You humiliated me in front of everyone.'

'How do you think I felt?' she spat back at him.

'Caitlyn!' She heard Axel yell and spied him racing across the road towards them.

He pressed a little harder. 'I would have dealt with Sophia,' he continued, his tone sinister. 'And I'm still going to. But you just *had* to hightail it out of there, making the people question my suitability, didn't you?'

'What do you expect the people to think when they find out you assaulted a woman?' Axel asked, shoving Andy off Caitlyn.

As soon as she was free, her hands instinctively rubbed her neck where his arm was pressing. She watched the exchange between Axel and her asshole ex-fiancé.

'Who the hell are you?' Andy growled. 'Do you know who I am?'

Axel shrugged. 'I'm the wrong guy to mess with, Andy Graeme,' he said. 'And you're the bastard who's going to leave right now before we call the cops.'

Andy swung a punch, but Axel ducked aside, making him hit the car instead. Andy shook his hand, crying out in pain. Axel checked the damage on the car before facing Andy again.

'*Dude*, you just dented my car!' he said, pointing to the dent.

Andy swung another punch, and Axel blocked it, grabbing onto his arm, and moving around Andy to pull his arm behind his back, pushing him against the car.

'I told you to *leave*, asswipe,' Axel growled in his ear, shoving him away from them again.

Andy pointed towards Axel as he backed away. 'You will hear from my lawyer,' he said.

'Oh, I agree,' Cameron said. 'Send Derek Small over for a visit, and I'll tell him exactly how you assaulted Miss Low without provocation. Your case would be squashed before you could say your own name.'

***

Axel brought a cup of tea over for her. She could feel her body shaking, but tried to keep her hands as steady as she could, taking the cup. She couldn't believe that Andy had treated her like that. Sure, he was never really a romantic or affectionate man, but he'd never hurt her before. Never threatened. Until now. But that's not what scared her the most. He'd said that he would deal with Sophia. What the hell did he mean by that?

But Axel—he had both comforted her and protected her in one long night. She had never asked him to do that, but there he was. And she knew that she shouldn't be having feelings for him and that what she felt for him now were romanticised feelings because of what he'd done for her. But she figured he didn't do it solely because of her. Surely, he would have done it for any woman that was in her position.

***

'I'll be back in a second,' Axel said as Caitlyn sipped from her tea.

What a mess the night had turned into. He didn't drop Caitlyn back at home because she wasn't ready to go back yet, and he thought she would be safe for now. Nothing like this ever happened in Goulburn, at least not that he'd heard of. He should have persisted, should have made her go home instead of staying in the car.

It had taken all of his restraint to not hit Andy Graeme. He wanted to. He wanted to watch him fall to the ground for even thinking of touching Caitlyn. He wondered if Cameron was right—Caitlyn might know something. And now, Cameron had her in his sights. He wouldn't be able to protect her from being questioned and being put in front of the jury to testify. And he wouldn't be able to avoid telling her what was going on anymore. He took a deep breath and entered Cameron's office, closing the door behind him.

'Caitlyn Low?' Cameron said. 'You had her with you and didn't tell me?'

'I didn't exactly know she was Andy Graeme's fiancée until last night,' he admitted.

'I told you we had to find her this morning,' Cameron added. 'You didn't tell me you already had her. We could have saved so much time and already had her in to answer our questions.'

'I already told you what happened.'

'What—that he'd cheated on her and got someone else pregnant?' Cameron asked. 'Wait, that actually happened?'

'Yes, it did,' Axel said. 'I don't know if she knows anything about Faith, or possibly those others, but I do know that *that* is the reason she didn't marry him.'

'We have to ask her.'

'The guy just assaulted her, Cameron,' Axel said, trying to keep his voice low enough that she wouldn't hear.

'Then there's no better time to ask her,' Cameron stated, standing to his feet and heading towards the door. 'She'd be mad at him enough to spill everything she knows.'

'She doesn't know we're working on Andy's case,' Axel said.

'You haven't told her?'

'I didn't want her to leave before we needed her,' he said.

Cameron squinted at Axel. 'How long have you known Caitlyn, Axel?'

'Remember the other day when I told you about a woman spilling the coffees on my shirt?' he asked. Cameron nodded. 'Well, that was her. That was the first time I saw her.'

Cameron rubbed his chin. 'And how did you find her again?'

He decided to skip telling Cameron about their interaction in the chemist. That one was more personal. 'Flop found her in the park. She was in her wedding dress and she was crying. I stopped to see if she was okay. She had nowhere to go, so I said that she could come back to my place to stay for a while and Tash could lend her some clothes.'

'Smooth,' Cameron teased.

'It's not like that,' he said, though he wished it might have been. 'I had no idea who she was at that stage, just her first name.'

Cameron raised his eyebrow. 'And you didn't tell me because you have feelings for her.' Axel's mouth tightened. 'Come on, Axel. You can't fool me. I have eyes and ears—I heard the tone in your voice when you called her name before racing out to act as her hero. You have to forget it, Axel. This is Andy Graeme's fiancée—'

'Ex-fiancée,' Axel corrected.

'You are treading on very thin ice if you plan on pursuing anything with Caitlyn Low, Axel.'

He knew that Cameron was right. He already knew that he was treading on thin ice with Caitlyn since the day they met. He knew that he shouldn't pursue anything with her—especially not while she's still in the rebound phase. He didn't think he could deal with that kind of messing around. But she was about to find out that he had been intentionally withholding the fact that he has been working on bringing Andy Graeme down for weeks which means that, if she had married that bastard, he would have been screwing with her life, too. And she would be hearing it from Cameron, not him.

*****

'How are you feeling, Caitlyn?' Cameron dragged a seat over to sit across from her.

'A little shaken,' she admitted. 'But better, thank you.'

Her eyes followed Axel as he pulled another chair over and sat next to Cameron. She wondered why he didn't just sit on the couch next to her. She might have felt a little more comfortable if he had.

'What's going on?' she asked, glancing back and forth between them.

Cameron leaned forward, resting his elbows on his knees. Axel stayed still, not taking his eyes off her. She couldn't read his expression, not fully. But there was the coolness in his eyes again.

'Caitlyn,' Cameron said. 'We're just going to be upfront with you. No beating around the bush.' He paused briefly before talking again. 'I'm sure you're aware that Andy Graeme has been going through a court case for the last month or so.'

She nodded. The legal case was all a misunderstanding, wasn't it? That's what Andy had told her. He'd said it would be over before long, then it dragged on for weeks. He'd never told her the details of it.

'Well, we're behind it,' Cameron said.

Her mouth dropped open. 'You mean—' She couldn't find the words.

'We represent the client who's suing him,' he continued.

She glanced back at Axel. His eyes were still on her, his lips pressed into a thin line, his brow furrowed. He hadn't told her. She'd thought it was the court case that had come between her and Andy in the first place, that had pushed him to sleep with Sophia. But then, she couldn't remember when the last time her and Andy had been intimate, anyway. Still, worrying about the court case had stressed her. And Axel should have told her as soon as he found out who she was. She focussed back on Cameron.

'And I know that it may have caused you some stress while you were with Andy,' Cameron added.

Caitlyn let out a laugh. 'That's a bit of an understatement.'

She stole another glance at Axel—his jaw had tightened.

'Caitlyn, are you aware of the nature of the case?' Cameron asked.

She shook her head. 'All he ever told me was that it was a misunderstanding.'

'It's not,' Axel said, his voice deep, sharp.

'Excuse me?' she said, shooting a look at Axel. His jaw was still tense, and he was keeping his focus on her.

'Caitlyn, he's being sued for aiding and abetting in the murder of at least one woman—Faith Jefferson,' Cameron said.

Faith. God, she hadn't heard her name in years. She shook her head, shaking back the tears. 'Impossible,' she said. 'Faith was killed in a car crash. Thank God they caught the guy who did it.'

'We have reason to believe that Andy was behind it,' Cameron said. The calmness with which he spoke only heightened how outlandish the accusation sounded.

'He wouldn't.' It came out before she had a chance to stop the automatic response.

'How do you know?' Cameron asked.

'Faith was my friend,' Caitlyn said, her eyes welling up. 'She was more than my friend. She was more like a sister to me all through school. We were closer than I ever was with Sophia. He knew how much she meant to me.'

'Did you know she was pregnant when she died?' Cameron asked.

Her mouth dropped open. Faith was pregnant? She had never known—Faith had never told her. She still had a few weeks to go in her degree. She knew that Faith was back home before her, but Caitlyn had cut off all outside contact to focus on her exams.

'Andy was the father,' Cameron said.

She shook her head. He knew what Faith meant to her—he wouldn't have done that, would he? But then, he'd done it with Sophia, and he was home at the same time as Faith. Heck, they went to the same university in Sydney, while Caitlyn was in Melbourne.

'No,' she whispered.

'I'm sorry that it's the first you're hearing about it, Caitlyn,' he continued. 'But I had it confirmed.'

Axel's head snapped up towards Cameron. Cameron shrugged at him. 'I made a few phone calls and pulled a favour so that they could get me the results today,' he explained, then looked back at Caitlyn. 'In fact, Faith wasn't the only one.'

'I don't understand,' she said.

She could feel her blood starting to boil, making the idea that she had just defended Andy stick in her throat. Andy had cheated on her more than once? And he'd got Faith pregnant as well as Sophia? And now, Cameron was saying there was more? If she'd known this earlier, she would have kicked him hard enough to actually cause some damage to him instead of pushing him off her.

'Those two other women from Sydney I talked to you about this morning, Axel,' he said. 'A genetics test was run on the babies at the time and the DNA was the same. Andy was the father.'

'What happened to them?' Caitlyn asked.

'One was about seven years ago,' Cameron said. 'The other about a year later. Both women went missing then were found dead some time later. They were both early on in the pregnancy.'

Caitlyn did the maths. Seven years ago, she was in Melbourne studying her degree and Andy was in Sydney studying his. And the bastard had cheated on her there, too. Her entire relationship with him was a lie.

'He was in Sydney,' she whispered.

'Were you with him, then?' Cameron asked, raising his eyebrow.

She stared at the floor. 'We'd been together for eight years,' she said. 'But we studied our degrees in that time. He was in Sydney, I was in Melbourne.' She shook her head, she just couldn't wrap her mind around it. 'But how does him being the father link him with their deaths?'

'He paid them, Caitlyn,' Axel said.

'What?' Paid them?

'Payments were made to a known drug dealer who seemed to have a hobby of killing people on the side,' Cameron explained. 'He was later arrested for their deaths. According to Faith's father, Andy tried to pay Faith to get an abortion and she sent the money back.'

'Faith didn't believe in abortions,' Caitlyn said. 'It was a touchy topic for her.'

'That's what her father said,' Cameron continued. 'Caitlyn, the same amount of money that he tried to send to Faith was sent to the man who is now serving time for her death.'

Oh, God. With this information, even she could see that it wasn't looking good for Andy. Could he really be behind their deaths? Did he have it in him? He'd never been much of a romantic before, but she'd never figured him to be someone to plan the demise of another person—especially because he got them pregnant. But then, he had never told her about any of the other women. And she was sure he would never have told her about Sophia if she hadn't overheard them talking. She felt the blood drain from her face. *Sophia*.

She hadn't realised that she'd said her name out loud.

'What about Sophia?' Axel asked.

'Who is Sophia?' Cameron asked. 'Is she the girl who he just got pregnant?'

She brought her gaze up to Axel. The coolness in his eyes was gone—the colour was sharp. 'If Andy did organise for that to happen to those women,' she said, trying to steady her voice. 'Does that mean she's in danger? Oh, God.' She clasped her hand over her mouth. 'He said that he was going to deal with her.'

Cameron was on his feet before she could blink, headed towards the office phone. 'Write down her address for me,' he said. 'I'll organise for protective custody, just in case.'

Chapter 11

It had been a long night. Axel dropped his keys in the bowl on the hall table near the door, closing the door behind Caitlyn. After discovering that Sophia could be in danger, Cameron had organised for the police to arrange protective custody for her. So far, Caitlyn hadn't cracked it at him. But it was late, and a lot for her to take in, and she still looked as though she was trying to process it all. Their drive home was silent. He had thought that she might have gotten straight into it, letting him have it for not telling her about it sooner. In fact, he still wouldn't have told her yet without being in a position where she had to find out—and she probably knew that, too.

Eight years. That's how long she had been with that bastard. That makes the estimated rebound time a long time. *Damn*. Not that she'd want to get with him in the end anyway. He was just providing a place to stay, some support, until she could get back on her feet. Now that he knows that she still cares about Sophia enough to care about her safety, maybe she would forgive her and move in with her. Maybe her family would realise she was right to not marry him when he's found guilty. Either way, Axel doubted that she would be staying here with him and his sister, and he wasn't sure he'd want her to stay. Without having a hope of anything further with her, he wasn't sure he'd be able to be around her. It wouldn't be good for him with his stress.

'Well, goodnight,' Caitlyn said, heading towards Tash's room.

And he couldn't work out how she must be feeling. Betrayed, he guessed, would be up there towards the top of the list. Hurt, probably. And most likely somewhat relieved that she managed to get out of locking herself into marriage with a potential psycho. She had almost reached the bedroom door when Axel noticed the pink hair scrunchie on the doorknob.

'Wait!' he said, whispering sharply. Her hand froze in the air. 'You can't go in there.'

'Why not?' she asked, squinting. 'This is my room while I'm here.'

'Not tonight,' he said, walking over to her, and flicking the scrunchie. 'Tash puts it on her doorknob when she doesn't want to be disturbed.'

'Maybe by you,' she said, reaching for the doorknob again. 'But my bed is in there, so I'm sure she won't mind me being in there.'

He stopped her hand before it got to the doorknob. 'Oh, but you might not like sleeping in there with her and Liam all night,' he said, teasing her.

She dropped her eyes and he followed her gaze to his hand holding hers. She didn't pull her hand back. She didn't flinch. And it made him want to touch her more, to lift her chin up and kiss her. But he couldn't. He let go of her hand and cleared his throat.

'Umm,' he said, struggling to find his words. 'You could stay in my bed tonight.'

Her eyes widened. 'Oh, ahh—'

'Oh, I'll sleep on the couch,' he added quickly. Maybe he should have thrown that little bit in with his suggestion to start with.

She exhaled, as though she'd been holding her breath. 'Are you sure?'

He smiled. 'Well, you didn't seem very happy about me staying in there with you,' he teased. 'So, I guess the couch will do fine.'

'Oh, stop it,' she said, whacking his arm. Her eyes were shining, and that smile he adored was back on her face. She followed him to his room. 'Do you have something I can wear, then, so I don't have to go disturb Tash and Liam?'

He went straight to his wardrobe and pulled out a clean t-shirt, passing it to her. 'You can wear this,' he said.

'Thanks,' she said.

She bit her lip nervously, and Axel thought it was one of the sexiest things he'd ever seen before. He had to get out of there now, or he wouldn't be leaving his room at all.

'Well, goodnight, then,' he mumbled, heading towards the door.

'Axel?' she said quietly. He turned to face her. God, she was making it hard for him to leave. She fidgeted with the shirt in her hands. 'You could have told me.'

He took a few steps towards her, then stopped so that he wouldn't get too close. He had to keep his resolve this time.

'About Andy,' she continued. She looked exhausted, worn out, and she sounded as though she had no energy to really let him have it. She sat on the edge of the bed, staring at her hands in her lap. 'And about you being on the prosecution team.'

'I didn't know half the things that Cameron said,' he said, finding himself sitting on the bed next to her. God, whatever happened to keeping control? 'And I thought you would have been mad if you found out that I was the one putting him through hell for weeks, especially if it was hard on you, too.'

'Oh, I would have been mad,' she said, looking up at him. 'I kind of still am.'

'But?' he said. He had a feeling that there was more to it, since she didn't exactly look like she was about to explode with fury.

'I don't know,' she said, looking back down at her hands. 'It was stressful for me. He never told me what it was about. He just said that he didn't want to stress me with details so close to the wedding, but I think it made it worse.'

'I'm sorry,' he said, wishing he could reach out and hold her hand. But he had to keep control. She made him feel things he shouldn't, and he had to push that aside.

'I guess if you told me before tonight,' she continued. 'I probably would have been madder. I wouldn't have believed you. But after what he did at the car—' She swallowed and looked back up at him, her eyes wide and round, searching his, a single tear rolling down her cheek.

His hand was on her cheek, his thumb wiping the tear away, before he could convince himself to keep control again. *Damn it*. She closed her eyes, her brow furrowed, and pressed her cheek against his hand even more.

'Like I said before,' he whispered. 'I'll take care of it. Cameron and I—we'll take care of it. And Andy will never get his filthy hands on you again, I promise.'

'You can't promise that,' she said, opening her eyes again—the most beautiful eyes he'd ever seen.

'Well, I'll be doing my very damned best to make sure he can't,' he said.

She smiled, a sweet smile. And he might have kissed her, if she had held his eyes for a moment longer. She turned her head away from him, then moved towards his bedside table.

'Axel,' she said, picking up the slot token that she'd given him with the coins for the coffee. 'Where did you find this?'

He rose to his feet so that he couldn't be tempted again to lay her on the bed. 'You gave it to me,' he said, smiling. 'In your generosity to buy me a fresh coffee that wasn't spilled on my shirt.'

Her smile was wide. 'I've been looking everywhere for it,' she said, rolling it around in her hand. 'I thought I'd never see it again.'

'Wait, you didn't mean to give it to me?' he asked. He'd thought that she gave it to him intentionally to mock him for asking her to buy him another coffee.

She shook her head. 'It was my grandfather's,' she said. 'He gave it to me before—' she cut off, glancing up at him. 'Well, before he passed. Thank you, for not throwing it out.'

'Well, I was going to keep it,' he said, extending his hand out towards her. 'I thought it was pretty cool. But I guess you can have it back—on one condition.'

'Oh?' she said, raising an eyebrow.

'You have to be nice to me,' he said.

She laughed. 'Might be hard,' she teased, standing up and starting to walk towards him. 'But I'm sure I could do that.'

He felt a smile pull at his lips. 'And you have to kiss me.' Wait, what?

'Is that so?' She moved closer.

He nodded. Why couldn't he stop? He turned his head and tapped his cheek with his finger. She stopped, inches away from him, and stood on her tippy toes to kiss his cheek. He turned his head, meeting her lips with his in a quick peck. A peck that made all time stop, if only for a moment. A peck that he hadn't planned to do. But then, it seemed he'd already lost all control and rational thought. She'd made him daring. She'd got inside his head and made him do things he wouldn't normally do.

She took a step back, her mouth open in surprise, a blush spreading on her cheeks. 'You are very cheeky, Mr Taylor,' she said, shaking her finger at him.

He raised an eyebrow. 'You liked it, Miss Low,' he teased.

Her blush darkened as she backed towards the bed. 'Goodnight, Axel,' she said, holding up the slot token. 'And thank you for the token.'

'Sweet dreams, princess,' he said, closing the door behind him.

As soon as the door was closed, he slapped his palm against his forehead. This woman had a hold on him that he shouldn't get used to. He didn't know what made him put the condition on giving the token back to her, or what made him steal that kiss, or even what made him call her *princess*—again. He'd been more than happy to give it back to her. And it made him smile that he'd managed to make her so frustrated at the café that she unintentionally gave him something that meant a lot to her.

But that kiss? It may have been short—too short, in his opinion—but it was sweet. And tender. And it made him hungry for more. And it was completely stepping out of bounds. But it was totally worth it. He moved towards the bathroom. Maybe he would find his restraint again in the shower—a cold one.

***

And she did have sweet dreams, very vivid ones at that. She could feel the soft tenderness of his kiss, sweet and gentle at first, then deeper—only a little—reminding her of what a first kiss should feel like. She could feel the butterflies in her stomach and the warmth of eagerness spreading across her body. She could taste the faint copper mixed with sweet mint as his tongue teased her lip before pressing deeper into the kiss.

Their mouths moved together, and she could feel the heat of his body as he lowered it against hers. She could feel his arousal pressing against her leg, even through their clothes. She wrapped her legs around him, pulling him closer. He broke his mouth free and moved his lips down her throat, leaving a trail of nips and kisses and focussing on the tender part of her neck where Andy had pressed his arm against her.

She would remember this dream in the morning, and mentally add it to her list of favourites. He kept kissing across her shoulder as his hands moved up her side, lifting her shirt as they moved.

'Mmm, Axel,' she said.

Her eyes shot open at the sound of her own voice, but the dream didn't disappear.

'Axel!'

He pulled away and his hands stopped moving. He studied her face.

'What?'

She saw the haze in his eyes clear up and he looked around them before focussing back on her.

'Oh, God!' he said, flinging himself off the bed—off her. She couldn't help but feel disappointed. 'I'm, umm,' he stammered, looking down at himself. He turned so that his back was towards her. 'Really sorry,' he managed. 'I thought I was dreaming. God! Could you just, ahh'—he pointed behind him towards the bedside table—'pass me the pills in the drawer, please?'

She reached into the drawer and found the container with the pills and passed it to him. He tipped one into his hand, put it in his mouth and swallowed it, screwing the cap back on and putting the container back on the bedside table, still with his back towards her.

'You can look,' she said, furrowing her brow. 'I'm decent.'

He dropped his head, his body tense. 'Oh, I'm not,' he said.

She smiled, studying the strong muscles on his back. He was wearing nothing but shorts, and he looked pretty damn fine. But she shouldn't be thinking that. She shouldn't be wanting to start anything with anyone so soon after things ended with Andy. But, in saying that, she was sure the relationship was over a long time ago—it was never really there. So, why shouldn't she want to start something with someone else? But Axel—they easily swung from being unable to get along to flirting in the same conversation. But they were from different worlds, and right now, she had no idea what her world was. It didn't stop her from finding him irresistible, though, and it was only a matter of time before all of her resolve disappeared.

He cleared his throat. 'Again, I am sorry,' he said. 'I sometimes sleepwalk when I'm stressed.'

'You were sleepwalking?' she teased.

He turned to face her. 'Are you mocking me?' he asked. 'Yes, I was sleepwalking. Obviously, since I wouldn't have done that if I wasn't.'

'Oh,' she said, feeling like she'd just been slapped.

She dropped her gaze to where her fingers traced the pattern on the doona, crossing her legs. She shouldn't feel disappointed, right? She shouldn't feel cut. She had just decided that they were from different worlds, that they wouldn't be able to be together anyway. But to think that *that* was only sleepwalking with no feelings at all—that hurt.

His eyes widened. 'Oh, no! I didn't mean it like that,' he said, sitting on the bed in front of her. He reached out and put his hand on hers. 'God, no. Caitlyn, I've wanted to. More than anything, I've wanted to. But I would never do it without making sure you're okay with it first. And the timing, Andy, the court case—it's all crazy at the moment. It just—'

'It wouldn't work,' she finished, looking up at him. His face dropped, and she wondered if he felt disappointed, too. 'We're from two different worlds, even if I don't know what mine is anymore.' She left out the fact that she'd wanted it, too.

He swallowed, and nodded slowly, removing his hand from hers. She wondered what he was actually going to say, but knew that she couldn't encourage anything between them.

'But you should stay with me,' she said. What happened to not encouraging it?

'What?'

'Well, there's room in this bed for the two of us,' she continued.

He shook his head. 'That's not a good idea,' he said.

'But sleeping on a comfortable bed helps relieve stress,' she said. 'And the couch is by no means as comfortable as a bed.'

'Do you want me to stay, Caitlyn?' he asked, catching her eyes with his.

She swallowed. She shouldn't say it—where was her restraint? Any amount of restraint.

'Yes, I do.'

Chapter 12

He wasn't there when she woke up. The blankets were pulled up next to her, straightened neatly, smelling faintly of him. Sure, they may not have done anything after their little bout of unintentional intimacy, but there's still that emptiness to be felt in waking up with the other person gone without even a goodbye. And she knew that she shouldn't feel that way. They shared a bed, so what? They stayed on their respective sides of the bed, backs turned to each other. Heck, there was even a pillow between them. She had overheard him talking to Cameron last night about being somewhere early this morning, but she still figured that he would have told her when he was headed off.

She could still feel the tenderness where his lips kissed hers, and she still felt the tingle that lingered wherever he touched. She shouldn't—she couldn't. But she'd wanted it, and she would never forget the way he made her feel when he was kissing her, even if he was still asleep. He wasn't asleep when he told her that he'd wanted to do that anyway. He wasn't asleep when he put his hand on hers or when he agreed to sleep in there with her. And that is what made her want it more.

She was about to get dressed in the clothes she'd worn last night because the clothes she was borrowing from Tash were in Tash's room, except that she couldn't find them. She did, however, find a new pair of blue jeans and a shirt on his desk with a note sitting on top. She read it.

Caitlyn,

I bought these for you when I bought my new shirt. Figured you might need something to wear that actually belonged to you. I hope they fit.

Axel.

She smiled at the note and took the clothes, putting them on. The jeans fit her perfectly. The shirt was slightly on the larger side, but it was comfortable. Besides, she preferred wearing slightly oversized shirts rather than skintight ones. Maybe the gesture filled that emptiness a little. It wasn't anything about last night, but it was still something. She felt the butterflies in her stomach when she read through the note again. Axel had thought of her. From what she knew, he didn't have much time yesterday to shop for anything other than a new shirt for himself. But now, he'd surprised her with a new set of clothes.

She made the bed and folded the shirt she'd slept in, then headed out to the kitchen to get some breakfast.

'You're just in time,' Tash said. 'I just boiled the jug. Do you want a coffee?'

'I'd love one,' she replied, grabbing a bowl and some cereal.

Tash pulled out a third cup and put some coffee into it. 'Sleep well?' she asked.

'It was—' she started, pausing for a moment. 'Good, I guess. It was late when we got back, and I had some strange dreams.' Well, one dream, which turned out to be actually happening. And it wasn't exactly what she would call strange. 'And my mind was elsewhere.'

'What were you thinking about?'

'Oh, just about the court case,' she said. It wasn't really a lie, since she was thinking about the court case, and how Andy acted at the car. But mostly about Axel and how he'd woken her up in the middle of the night rather passionately.

'Axel told you about it?' Tash asked, handing her a coffee.

'You know?'

Tash shrugged. 'He tells me just about everything. I knew about the court case before he met you, though.'

'Oh,' she replied. 'Well, he didn't really have much of a choice. Andy showed up and kind of … threatened me, I guess.'

Tash's eyes widened. 'Are you okay?'

'I was a bit shaken up,' she replied. 'But I'm okay. And Axel and Cameron explained everything to me. I couldn't believe it at first, but I'm not exactly surprised. He was never really into romance, so it kind of makes sense that he could have been doing other stuff on the side.' Like sleeping with other woman and organising their demise.

'It'd be a lot to take in, I'm sure,' Tash replied, picking up the other cups and walking towards the lounge room. She stopped before she walked through the archway. 'Oh, I saw Axel walking out of his room this morning, did he sleep in there with you last night?'

She nodded, trying to think of an excuse but coming up empty.

'So, are you guys like, a thing, now?' Tash asked, a coy smile on her face.

Caitlyn blushed. 'No,' she said, not entirely convincing herself. 'But we're friends.'

'Friends don't sleep together,' Tash teased.

'They can if it's just that—sleep,' Caitlyn said. 'Besides, I wasn't going to share your room with you and Liam.'

'So, you're telling me that nothing happened?' Tash asked, smiling.

'That's exactly what I'm saying,' she said.

Tash squinted. 'You know, I could have sworn I heard you moan his name,' she said, winking. 'Must have been imagining it.'

Caitlyn's blush deepened, and she turned her head to focus on the cereal bowl. 'You were definitely imagining it.'

'How interesting,' Tash said, heading into the lounge room.

Interesting, indeed.

***

'Damn it!'

Cameron flung the door to their office open. Axel followed behind him, a little fazed over how the morning visit with Faith's killer went.

'I don't get why he refused to talk,' he said.

'You don't get it?' Cameron asked, frustrated. 'Because Andy Graeme is holding something over him! He's never going to talk if he's being blackmailed.'

'I figured he'd be more than ready to talk since he's already serving time,' Axel said, sitting on the couch. He stared at the floor. It had made sense to him—if the guy's in prison already, he should, theoretically, be willing to talk to bring down the person that got him there in the first place. He rested his head on his hands.

'The guy didn't even come to the visitation room, Axel,' Cameron said, pulling a chair over to sit opposite him. 'Don't think that prisoners are exempt from being blackmailed. You might be surprised to find out just how many are.'

'So, what's that mean? That Andy Graeme got to him first?' Axel looked up at him. 'How do we get him to talk?'

'I don't know,' Cameron said, rubbing his temple. 'But we need to come up with a plan. Have you asked Caitlyn to testify, yet?'

'I didn't get a chance,' Axel said.

'Well, you need to find a chance,' Cameron said. 'At the moment, she's our only hope. But that's not the only problem we have.'

'And here I thought it couldn't get worse,' Axel said.

'Oh, it could get a lot worse, but it's not going to,' Cameron said. 'Sophia refused protective custody.'

'What?' Axel couldn't believe it. Caitlyn would be devastated if he told her that Sophia could be back in danger. 'Why would she refuse it?'

'Because she doesn't think she's in any danger,' Cameron said.

'Can we still get her protective custody if she refuses?'

Cameron shook his head. 'We can't do anything for her unless she wants it.'

They sat in silence for a moment, Cameron rubbing his eyes, Axel staring at the floor. He'd thought that visiting Allen Muller, Faith's convicted killer, would have been a sure thing.

If he'd known that the guy wasn't even going to bother seeing them, he might have stayed in bed a bit longer. Maybe he could have given the clothes to Caitlyn himself instead of leaving a note, and maybe he could have even had some breakfast before leaving. He'd considered waking Caitlyn up before he left, but he'd felt her tossing and turning all night and, when he would have woken her, she was fast asleep. She needed the sleep. According to Tash, she had been tossing and turning all night when she slept on the mattress in her room. He just didn't have the heart to take any amount of peaceful sleep from her.

But deciding not to wake her didn't mean that he couldn't kiss her cheek—softly, of course, so she wouldn't disturb—or gently brush the hair away from her face, or straighten the blankets and tuck her in. Even if nothing intentional happened last night, he still couldn't help but imagine how it would feel seeing her in his bed every morning. And he liked the picture. But he knew that it was just a romanticised idea. Like she'd said, it wouldn't work. But he wished it would.

'We need to talk.'

Axel and Cameron both shot their eyes towards the man standing at the door. How had they not heard him come in?

'You shouldn't be here,' Cameron said, standing up, but not moving towards the man.

'No one knows I'm here,' the man said solemnly. 'I have something that might be of help to you in your case against Andy.' He held up a small recorder.

Cameron looked at the recorder. 'Why would you want to help us?' he asked.

'Because he messed up,' the man said. 'And he needs to pay for the wrongs he's done, even if it breaks my heart to say it.'

Cameron nodded at the man, then looked at Axel. 'Axel, meet Hank Graeme,' he said, looking back at the man. 'Andy's father.'

***

'Let's hear it,' Cameron said as the three of them gathered around Cameron's desk.

Hank pressed the play button and placed the recorder on the desk and they all listened.

'How do you know what the case is about?' Andy said.

'You forget that Derek Small is my lawyer, too,' Hank said. 'He's handling all of our family matters, and *this* is a family matter, since our finance records show money being sent off to suspicious accounts.'

'It's none of your business.'

'Did you do it?'

'Do what?' Andy asked.

'Arrange Faith's death.'

Andy laughed. 'Of course I didn't,' he said. 'The guy was just supposed to rough her up, scare her into getting rid of it. How was I to know he was going to kill her? Worked out for the better anyway.'

'And the others?' Hank asked. 'Did you arrange for them to be killed?'

'They weren't anyone important.'

'You took their lives!'

'I was just dealing with the problems like you dealt with the girl nine years ago,' Andy said.

'Dealing with the problems would be not getting into it in the first place,' Hank said, his voice raised. 'And I didn't take her life like you did with those girls.'

'No, you paid someone to do it for you,' Andy said. 'I just followed in your footsteps.'

'I dealt with that girl by paying her out to move away and keep it quiet,' Hank said. 'And by continuing to send monthly payments to support her and her child.'

'What?' Andy said, his tone sounding a little nervous.

'I have never killed anyone, Andy,' Hank said. 'You have crossed a line.'

The recording stopped playing and Axel looked up at Hank, then over at Cameron. This was a recording of Andy admitting to hiring someone to deal with the girls he got pregnant—that there were more than one. And they couldn't use it.

'Hank, this is—' Cameron said, pausing briefly. 'Helpful, for us. Now we know for sure that we're on the right track. But it's inadmissible in court.'

'It's a confession, how could that be inadmissible?' Hank asked, shaking his head.

'It was recorded without Andy's permission,' Axel explained. 'As far as the court is concerned, that conversation never happened.'

'But he can't be allowed to get away with doing that,' Hank said, taking a seat, staring at the desk.

'He did that to those poor girls. I can't let him do it to anymore. He needs to be stopped and he won't listen to me. He's too stubborn.'

'Oh, we agree,' Cameron said. 'We just need to get evidence that has been legally obtained.'

'Like what?' Hank asked.

'Well, someone to testify against him would be a good start,' Cameron said. 'Preferably someone who was involved with it.'

'Like Allen Muller?' Hank asked, glancing up at them.

'He was our first choice,' Cameron said, shrugging. 'But he refused to see us when we went to talk to him this morning.'

Hank stared back at the desk, squinting. 'What if I can get him to talk?'

Chapter 13

'What do you mean Sophia refused protective custody?' Caitlyn asked.

'She doesn't think she's in danger,' Axel explained to her, taking a sip from his cup of tea.

She leaned back against the couch where she was sitting next to Axel, watching the pictures flashing across the television screen. If Sophia had refused protective custody, that meant that she could be in danger at any time. Caitlyn was sure that, even though Sophia didn't seem to think so, Andy was capable of hurting her like he did to those other women. Unfortunately, those other women got the worse end of it.

Axel had told her about the recording. He'd told her that there were three other women before

Faith—one who was still alive and being looked after with payments from Andy's father, Hank, and two who are now dead. He'd told her that Andy had said on the recording that Faith was only supposed to be roughed up, scared into getting an abortion. But she'd never believed in that. What went wrong? What happened that got Faith killed?

She wondered why Hank had come forward to help bring Axel down, but wasn't overly surprised at the same time. Hank had always had his ethical code that he believed in. He'd been known to stretch the rules on occasion, but he'd always done the right thing. But providing evidence against your own son? She wondered if she would ever be able to do that if she was in his situation. She would probably feel terrible about it. But then, Andy and his father had never had a very close relationship.

'Is she?' Caitlyn asked.

Axel shrugged. 'I don't know,' he said, leaning back, stretching his arm across the back of the couch.

She could feel the warmth of his arm across her shoulders, even though he wasn't touching her, and wondered how it would feel to lean against him. Would he put his arm around her? But she didn't have the nerve to find out. She couldn't encourage something that wouldn't work. She pulled the slot token out of her pocket and rolled it between her fingers, wishing that her grandfather was still here. He would know what to do. He would help her.

'I hope she'll be okay,' she said.

'I thought you were mad at her.' He nudged her shoulder with his hand.

She felt a shiver run down her spine from his touch. 'I am,' she said, trying to shake the feeling off. 'But she was still my best friend for so many years. It's hard not to worry about her when she could be in trouble.'

He smiled at her. 'That's what I like about you,' he said.

Caitlyn blushed. 'What?'

'You really are caring,' he said. 'Even if you are a hothead.'

'I am not a hothead!' she said, turning in her seat and frowning at him.

'Oh, is that just with me, is it?' he teased.

'Must be,' she mumbled, turning away again.

She looked down at the token in her hands to hide her blush. She remembered her grandfather saying to her that she had her grandmother's temper. He always said that her grandmother never had a temper with anyone except him.

'What's the story with that?'

'Hmm?' She looked up at Axel.

He nudged his eyes towards her hands. 'The slot token,' he said.

'Oh,' she said, looking back at the token. 'It was my grandfather's.'

'You've said that,' he said. 'Is there a story with it?'

Caitlyn smiled. The only person she'd ever told the story to was Sophia. She didn't think that Andy even knew how she got it. 'He used to gamble—a lot,' she hesitated a moment before continuing, deciding Axel could be trusted with the story. 'He was addicted to it and just saw that he was wasting money on it. So, he gave it up and never set foot in the casino again.'

'Was that the token where he decided to give it up?' he asked.

Caitlyn shook her head. 'He'd had a terrible day,' she continued. 'He'd just lost his brother in an accident. They were close, and he'd helped my grandfather quit gambling. But out of his old habit, he went to the casino and sat in front of the machine with this token in his hand for half an hour. He was debating whether to do it. He thought that, if he refused to put it in the machine, that he wouldn't get hooked again. But on the other hand, he figured that one token in the slot machine wouldn't hurt.'

'So, I take it he decided not to do it?'

Caitlyn smiled. 'He was about to put it into the machine when a woman who worked there stopped his hand and told him that he didn't have to do it,' she said. 'She'd been watching him while he was sitting there and could see the battle he was struggling with.' She paused, taking a breath. 'In that moment, he knew he'd just met the love of his life.'

'So, that woman was—'

'My grandmother,' she finished. 'He always said that life is a gamble and throws all kinds of curveballs at you. He told me that if he had never previously been addicted to gambling, and if his brother hadn't passed away that day, he wouldn't have been sitting at that slot machine with this token in his hand for so long, and he would never have met my grandmother.'

Axel swept her fringe away from her eyes, tucking her hair behind her ear and slowly brushing the back of his fingers against her cheek. She looked into his eyes that were filled with warmth and searching hers. She thought she could see something else in his eyes—desire? Wanting? Or maybe it was the reflection of her own wanting that she felt.

'That's a very sweet story. Thank you for sharing it with me,' he said.

His voice was deep, reverberating through her body, sending her hairs on edge. His fingers still brushed against her cheek, following her cheek bone, and rounding down below her ear to trace her jawline.

'It was meant to be,' she whispered.

She always loved to think that everything happened for a reason. Her grandfather would never have met her grandmother if he hadn't been through so much. And she would never have met Axel if she hadn't been about to marry Andy. With every inch of skin that his fingers brushed against as they moved from her jaw to the back of her neck, the fact that they were from two different worlds was rapidly becoming an inadequate excuse.

***

He fought against every nerve in his body that was trying to push him closer to her. It was a combination of exhaustion, common ground, loneliness, and attraction—it had to be. To make him question their unsuitability with 'why the hell not?' and to think that maybe, just maybe, their worlds weren't so different after all. But there was still so much that made them incompatible. But Axel didn't care about any of that right now. He had his hand at the back of her neck, he could easily pull her towards him and plant a kiss on those luscious lips. It wasn't fair that his unconscious self got more action than he does. He could still taste her on his lips and he wanted more.

Her eyes were searching his. Wide, round, inviting. He swallowed, holding back. There was still too much in the air to get involved. She'd so easily walked into his life, she could just as easily leave it and he would be the one that got hurt because she would be too easy to fall for. She *was* too easy to fall for. He heard Tash clear her throat, dropped his hand from the back of Caitlyn's neck, and looked up behind them to see Tash and Liam standing there.

'Hate to interrupt'—Tash waved her hand in front of her in a circular motion—'whatever this is. But we have an announcement to make.'

'You're pregnant?' he teased.

'What? No,' Tash said. 'Pregnant? Seriously?'

He shrugged. 'Seems to be the flavour of the day.'

'Well, no,' she replied. 'I'm not pregnant. But I am moving out.'

'What?'

Tash had been living with him for years. She always knew how to help him deal with his stress, not to mention she was always around for a chat since he didn't have time to catch up with friends outside of work. Not that he really had friends outside of work, he'd come to realise, other than Tash and Liam. But Tash was related, so she was kind of stuck with him.

'Liam and I have decided that it's time to get serious,' she continued. 'So, we're moving in together.'

'Tash, that's great,' Caitlyn said, getting up to give Tash a hug.

Axel watched as the two girls embraced each other. 'Yeah, great,' he said, not entirely enthused. He didn't fancy the idea of having to find another housemate. 'You didn't want to move in here, Liam?'

'Oh, I tried,' Liam joked.

'It'd be too crowded here, idiot,' Tash said.

Axel spread his arms out. 'It's just us.'

'There are two bedrooms,' Tash said.

'It's never been a problem before,' he said.

'There's four of us,' Tash said. As if on cue, Flop trekked into the room and jumped onto Axel's lap. 'And a dog,' she added.

'Wait, Caitlyn?'

Caitlyn turned to face him, before looking back at Tash.

'Yes, *Caitlyn*,' Tash said. 'Unless you guys plan to be shacking up, we should really be having another room. Either way, you wouldn't need us around if Caitlyn's here.'

'We're not shacking up,' he said.

'Oh, I'm not staying,' Caitlyn said at the same time.

He looked at Caitlyn. He thought he could see a tinge of pink on her cheeks, probably from Tash's smartass comment. But he didn't know why he was disappointed to hear those words leave Caitlyn's mouth. He never figured that Caitlyn would be staying forever, of course. Eventually, she would find her roots again and move on. He'd figured it wouldn't be long after the court case that it would happen. Her family would find that she was right to leave Andy—that she'd narrowly escaped being tied with a criminal. And she would fit right back in.

And when that happened, he would be left alone in this house with Flop. Not that it should bother him. He was a grown man, after all. It was just sad to think that they were coming to the end of an era.

'So, you've found somewhere else to go?' Tash asked, drawing her attention to Caitlyn.

'Well, no,' Caitlyn stammered. 'But staying here was only supposed to be temporary.'

'So, now it can be permanent,' Tash said. 'Since there will be an extra room.'

Axel felt his mouth drop open. He quickly closed it.

'Oh, I don't think Axel would want me staying here getting into all of his puzzles,' Caitlyn teased, dropping her gaze to the floor.

Was she avoiding looking at him? He didn't blame her. Moving in with him would be a terrible idea. He was already struggling enough to keep his hands off her in the few days she'd been here, how would he be expected to control himself with her moving in? Really, the sooner this was all over and the sooner she was gone, the better. They could go back to their normal lives and carry on as usual. But he knew that his life could never return to normal after meeting her. He would never be able to forget her.

'Isn't that right, Axel?' Tash asked.

'What?' He hadn't realised that he'd zoned out during the conversation while staring at Caitlyn.

'I said that you would think that Caitlyn should stay, since she has nowhere to go, don't you?' Tash said, her eyes widening as if she was trying to tell him something.

'Yeah, sure,' he said.

'That doesn't sound very convincing,' Caitlyn said quietly.

'You should stay.'

She glanced up at him, her eyes a warm violet, and he knew that he shouldn't have agreed to it. But what was he supposed to say? That he didn't want her staying with him? Especially if Tash and Liam aren't around? Frankly, the idea was both appealing and terrifying at the same time. At least he wouldn't have to look for another housemate. But he had to remember that Caitlyn was just that—his housemate. They couldn't be more because, sooner or later, she would leave. And he wouldn't be able to stop her.

'So, it's settled,' Tash said. 'Caitlyn is officially moved in, and I will be out by the end of the day.'

Axel swallowed as Caitlyn smiled at him. It was definitely a bad idea.

Chapter 14

Caitlyn bent down into a stretch that looked and felt somewhat like a pretzel. She could hear the birds singing outside as the first rays of sun shone through the window, hitting the patterns on the rug in front of her. It all felt surreal, being able to call this place her home now. It didn't take much for Tash to move out last night. She packed most of her clothes in a suitcase and her roomful of things and took them over to Liam's place, leaving a few sets of clothes for Caitlyn to use.

Admittedly, Tash's bed was more comfortable than the mattress on the floor, but it still wasn't as comfortable as Axel's bed. And that was what kept her up for most of the night—Axel. He was sleeping in the room next to her, supposedly stress-free. He'd taken Flop in with him, she guessed to keep him company enough to maybe make sure he didn't sleep walk. He hadn't seemed too convincing about her officially moving in with him while Tash moved out. And she had no idea why she even agreed to do it. She'd never been one to make rash decisions, yet in the last few days, she'd made more than she thought she'd made in her life.

Tash had a point—she still had nowhere to go. And she didn't know when she would have somewhere else to go. She might have thought that she would have when the court case is over, but seeing her mother the other day made her think otherwise. Even if her family did realise that she'd done the right thing, she didn't think she wanted to go back there. But she had to work out what she would do. At least she never quit her job, like Andy had wanted her to do. She could take her time off to work out what she wanted to do and still have a job to go back to. At least it was paid leave—too bad she didn't have her purse.

So, with Tash moving out, and being offered the extra room, she figured it would be all right. But now, she wasn't so sure. How could she think that she would be able to live with Axel and not feel for him? She was already having a hard time squashing the feelings that were growing for him. Especially when he touched her the way he did last night and looked at her with those eyes. Every time she saw him, she could feel her resolve slipping further out of reach. She just had to try harder. She pulled herself out of the pretzel and moved into a downward dog, almost falling over when Axel opened his door and Flop bounced over to her, licking her face. She sat on the ground, Flop climbing into her lap and looked up at Axel who had a cheeky grin on his face.

'Sleep well, homie?' she said, instantly regretting her choice of words.

'Homie?' he teased.

'Ahh, yes,' she replied, trying desperately to cover it up. 'You know, since we're housemates now.'

He shook his head. 'Mmm, that's not going to happen,' he said, walking towards the kitchen.

She jumped to her feet and followed him. 'Oh, but it could be fun,' she said, watching him spoon some coffee into a takeaway mug and putting the kettle on.

He laughed. 'I don't do *homie*,' he said, waving the mug in front of him in a mocking gesture. 'How about Law Dude and'—he paused, squinting at Caitlyn—'Yoga Pants.'

'*Yoga Pants*?'

'Don't mock the pants,' he teased, pouring some boiling water into his cup. 'Just remember that you started the whole nickname thing, *homie*.'

'Ha!' she said. 'See? You're warming up to it.'

'It's not happening,' he said, smiling.

He was standing so close to her. She could smell that woody scent of his cologne mixed with soap, though it was stronger now, not faint like it was when she bumped into him at the café. The strong aroma of his coffee wafted up towards her and she felt her insides stir. He was clean-shaven, his hair still wet. When had he snuck to the bathroom? She hadn't heard or seen him go, but then, she had only been doing her yoga for a short time before he came out.

His smile widened, and she could see the glint of the sunlight on his teeth. She reminded herself to breathe and felt even shorter than him than she thought she was—probably because he was wearing his shoes and she was only wearing socks on her feet. But their height difference felt like a perfect height. Andy had only been a little taller than her and she'd always wished he was taller. She always liked the idea of her man being tall enough that she could wear heels and he would still be taller. But she couldn't think that about Axel—he was her housemate now. Thinking like that would just make things complicated.

She took a step back, feeling her lower back rest against the edge of the kitchen counter. Without taking his eyes off hers, he followed, his body still only a few inches from hers. She could feel the heat of his body through his clothes and felt her head spinning, her breath catching in her throat. She felt her lips part, relaxing, waiting, even though she tried to convince herself that she didn't want it. It felt as though he was searching her, his eyes looking deeply into hers, and she could feel the sparks flying between them. If they weren't careful, those sparks could start a raging fire.

'Axel,' she whispered.

He reached behind her, his arm brushing against her shoulder, and pulled his hand back, holding up the lid of the coffee cup between them. Her mouth dropped open. He was just reaching for the lid? And she'd thought … she stopped herself. She couldn't think anything. She couldn't let herself think anything. He backed up, heading towards the door with his coffee.

'I'm off,' he said, reaching down to give Flop a scratch.

'Wait, you're leaving already?' Caitlyn asked, following him towards the door.

'I have to get to work,' he said, shrugging.

'I was hoping we'd get to talk, maybe have a coffee before you left,' she said. She'd wanted to see if he really was okay with her staying here, and she also wanted to talk about Sophia.

'I'm sorry, I don't have time,' he said, furrowing his brow.

She bit her lip and dropped her gaze to the floor. It was earlier than she thought he had to be at the office. Was he avoiding her? She knew saying that she'd stay was a bad idea.

'I'm not avoiding you, Caitlyn,' he said, as if reading her thoughts. She lifted her gaze and caught his eyes. 'We're going back over to the prison. Hank seems to think that he can get Allen Muller to talk, so we're going to see him—again.'

'I get it,' she said. 'The hearing is coming up, so you have to give it a lot of time. I'm just still concerned about Sophia. She should really have accepted the protective custody.'

'I agree,' he said. 'She should have.'

'I was thinking that I might be able to convince her into accepting it.' Thinking about Sophia was the other thing that kept her up for most of the night. 'That is,' she said, 'if I could get in touch with her, or maybe see her at her home.'

'Sure,' he said. 'I'll drive you to her place later and wait out the front, just in case.'

'That would be great,' she said. She was nervous about seeing Sophia, since she was still mad. But she knew that the only person who could convince her into getting the protective custody was her.

'Oh, about the hearing,' he said, hesitantly. 'Cameron wants to know if you'll testify.'

'What?'

'I know you didn't know about his being involved with the other girls, but,' he explained. 'He *did* assault you, and you can testify on that because it shows that he isn't what he appears to be.'

'Do I really have a choice?' she asked.

Testifying at the hearing isn't exactly what she wanted to do. She didn't plan on intentionally putting herself in a situation where she had to look at that bastard again. But maybe it would be for one last time.

He shrugged. 'Cameron will probably subpoena you if you don't.'

She knew she didn't have a choice.

***

While he waited in the visitation room with Cameron, Axel's eyes kept drooping. He straightened himself in his chair in an attempt to make himself less comfortable—not that these chairs were overly comfortable to start with. He felt as though the little bit of sleep he managed to get last night was pure napping and not very restful. He still couldn't believe that Tash had moved out so quickly. Her and Liam had only just announced it, then within a few hours she was out, her room officially assigned to Caitlyn.

Caitlyn, the beautiful woman he was increasingly struggling to resist with every second that she was near him. He'd tried to stay quiet this morning, sneaking out to the bathroom to have his shower. She was still out of sight when he had returned back to his room and closed his eyes in one last attempt to get any sleep. He figured it must have been his subconscious, keeping him awake. He didn't want to sleepwalk again, not after last night. He didn't think he'd ever lost control like that while sleepwalking. But then again, he'd never had a beautiful woman sleeping in his bed for him to lose control like that.

And then, seeing her doing her yoga when he came out of his room, every image of her that he'd imagined and every urge that he'd tried to push to the back of his mind, had crept back over him. He'd planned it well, or so he thought—he'd planned to only be leaving his room with enough time to get a coffee and head off to the prison so that he wouldn't have to talk to her. It's not that he wanted to avoid her, he just knew he wouldn't want to leave if he did get in a conversation with her. He hadn't planned on her being ready to pounce with conversation so early. She had been talking faster than his morning mind could even think.

She looked cute, wearing her yoga pants, a hoodie, and her hair in plaits. He'd wanted to tuck the few stray hairs behind her ears and kiss away the disappointed look on her face when he said he had to leave. He didn't know what he was thinking when she stood between him and the lid of his coffee cup. He'd seen the look in her eyes and he'd felt the heat passing between them. He could still smell her scent—sweet, though not of the apple and cinnamon that she smelled of when they first met, but rather a sweet vanilla. He'd wanted to see if her lips tasted the same as she smelled, and he'd felt that she wouldn't have stopped him from kissing her. But he'd also known that he wouldn't be able to stop himself if he did. It wouldn't have just been a simple kiss.

Axel tried to shake his thoughts from his tired mind. Here he was, sitting in the visitation room of the prison, about to question an inmate in hopes that they'll be able to convict Andy Graeme, and all he could think about was the stunningly irresistible woman he'd left at home doing the downward dog with only Flop for company.

'She'll do it,' he whispered to Cameron.

'What?'

'Caitlyn will testify,' he said. 'She didn't know anything about his affairs and involvement, but she will testify that he assaulted her and said that he would deal with Sophia.'

'Perfect,' Cameron said. 'Now, all we need is for this guy to talk.'

As if on cue, Allen Muller was let into the room and took a seat at the table opposite them. He looked at Axel, then over to Cameron.

'Morning, Mr Muller,' Cameron started. 'I'm Cameron Landon, this is Axel Taylor.'

'I know who you are,' Allen said. 'Hank told me I'm to tell you what really happened, but I don't fancy what will happen when his son finds out, so let's get it over with.'

Axel glanced over at Cameron who seemed undeterred by his response. 'Well, start talking,' Cameron said, hitting the record button on the video camera.

'It was an accident,' Allen started.

'It was ruled intentional,' Cameron said.

'But it wasn't,' Allen continued. 'I was paid to rough her up a little, you know—scare her into getting an abortion. I saw her get into her car when I was heading over to see her, so I followed her. She was driving a while and I eventually realised that she must have noticed I was following her and was trying to shake me off. She started doing things like slowing down, then going faster. She—'

He paused, looking away from them. When he looked back, his eyes were watery.

'He started ringing me to see if it had been done. She tried to get away by pretending as though she was going to take a left turn, then spun right,' he continued. 'She lost control while I was reaching for the phone and I–I crashed into her. They said she died instantly.'

'Who paid you?' Cameron asked.

Allen paused, his eyes passing between Axel and Cameron. 'Andy Graeme did,' he said. 'I wasn't supposed to kill her—it was an accident. But he said that it was better that she was dead anyway. He said it meant that she could never talk and that it seemed to be the thing that works. That's why he wanted me to kill the next one.'

'Wait, what next one?' Axel asked, leaning forward. They'd seen the extra payment on the finance records made to Allen's account.

'You don't know?' Allen asked, his eyes wide. 'Jessie Turner. Happened about two years ago.'

'So, you're saying that you killed another girl for Andy Graeme?' Cameron asked, leaning onto the table.

'Oh, I didn't kill her,' Allen said. 'Andy Graeme wanted me to, but I couldn't bring myself to end someone else's life on purpose. I thought if I could get her to disappear it would be okay. When I found her, she begged me not to hurt her and she was crying. She had a bruise on her arm and said that he had tried to force her to change her opinion on getting rid of it. She'd just miscarried when I got there and promised she wouldn't tell anyone. I let her go and told Andy that I'd dealt with it.'

'So, Jessie Turner is still around?' Axel asked. If they could find her …

'Unless something has happened to her,' Allen replied. 'As far as I know, she is. But I'd have no idea where—she left town.'

'Mr Muller,' Cameron said. 'We're going to need you to testify in court.'

Cameron stopped recording, and they waited until Allen had been led from the room before speaking. Axel turned to Cameron, rubbing his eyes.

'So, what's the next part of the plan?' he asked.

Cameron smiled. 'We find Jessie Turner.'

'And how do you plan on doing that, Cameron?' Axel asked.

'I have my ways,' Cameron said, raising his eyebrow. 'And he goes by the title of Private Investigator.'

Chapter 15

'You got him to confess?'

'Well, technically, Hank got him to confess,' Axel said.

Caitlyn stared at the dashboard in front of her. She still couldn't believe that Hank Graeme was really on their side and that he'd manage to, somehow, convince Allen Muller to talk. And she still couldn't believe that Andy had been behind Faith's death. They had been good friends and she was still doing exams at university when Faith died. She'd never known that she was pregnant. But Faith was still in the past—even if her memory was still very much alive. And Caitlyn had to focus on the person who really could be in danger now.

'Thank you for bringing me to Sophia's,' she said, looking up at Axel.

'I get it,' he said. 'Like I said, you are a caring person, even if you're mad at the person because they basically screwed you over.'

'Way to encourage me to go in and talk to her,' she replied, glancing over at Sophia's front door. She just had to find the motivation and courage to get out of the car and go to her door. Then to knock.

'Sophia could be in danger,' Axel said, 'and you are the only one who could possibly talk her into agreeing to the protective custody.'

'You're right,' she mumbled, still hesitating to leave.

'On another note. You're no longer listed as being missing, so your talk with your mother must have worked.'

'Or Andy called it off, since he found me in the car the other night,' she said, looking back at him.

'Either way,' he said, shrugging. 'No one is looking for you or your kidnapper.' He pointed to his chest. 'And I'll be right here, so you have nothing to worry about. So, what are you waiting for?'

Caitlyn sighed, and climbed out of the car, pausing for a moment before making her way towards Sophia's front door. Honestly, talking to Sophia was one of the last things she wanted to do. But she had to. She couldn't live with herself if she found out that something happened to Sophia when she had a chance to protect her. She was mad at Sophia now, but she might not be forever. One day, she might forgive her, and they might go back to normal—well, as close to normal as they could. That wouldn't be today, but she didn't want to rule out any opportunity to forgive her by not helping her when she needed it.

As much as she would like to put off seeing her, time was the enemy right now. She stood at the door, took a deep breath, and knocked. Then, she knocked again. There was still no answer. So, she knocked a third time, calling her name as she did.

'Sophia? Are you home?'

She was about to turn and head back to the car when the front door wedged open and Sophia peeked out.

'Caitlyn? What are you doing here?' Her voice sounded rushed.

Sophia opened the door wider for Caitlyn to walk through, glancing out the door nervously before closing it. Caitlyn turned to face her, her mouth dropping open when she saw the bruises on Sophia's wrists.

'Soph, what happened?' she asked, lifting Sophia's hands into the light to get a better look.

Sophia pulled her hands away from Caitlyn and tugged at her sleeves to cover her wrists.

'It's nothing,' she said.

Caitlyn studied her ex-best friend. Her eyes were reddened and swollen and she looked weary, sore, scared. Caitlyn put her hand to her own neck which still ached from the pressure Andy had put against it.

'Did Andy do that?' she asked.

Sophia glanced at anything other than Caitlyn. 'He didn't mean to, I'm sure,' she said quietly, as if trying to convince herself.

'No,' Caitlyn said, taking Sophia by the shoulders. 'Don't tell yourself that.'

'He's been stressed, that's all,' Sophia continued. 'He told me he's being sued and said that it's stressing him. I thought he'd be excited about the—' She broke off, glancing up at Caitlyn, her eyes welling up.

'The baby, Sophia, you can say it,' Caitlyn said, even though she felt the burn in her throat as she said it.

Sophia started sobbing, the tears running freely now. 'I'm so sorry, Caitlyn,' she said. 'I never meant to hurt you, I swear. It was late, and I was lonely, and I came over to see if you were home, but you were at work. He invited me in and we had some drinks and it just ... I'm so, so sorry.'

Caitlyn swallowed, her body numb. She clenched her teeth. She hoped that they wouldn't have to talk about this yet, she wasn't ready for that conversation. She had come here to convince her to take the protective custody, but she was struggling to convince herself to try.

'I don't want to talk about that,' she forced out, hoping that she could hold it together.

Sophia wiped her eyes. 'What do you mean?' she asked. 'I thought you'd be mad at me.'

'I am, Sophia, but I'm not ready to talk about that.'

'Then why did you come?' Sophia asked, her sobbing easing.

'The protective custody,' Caitlyn forced out. There, she'd mentioned it. Now, she had no choice but to keep talking about it. 'Why did you refuse it?'

'I didn't think I needed it,' Sophia said, leaning against the door. 'Andy's not that kind of person.'

'Yeah, well, I thought that too,' Caitlyn said, rubbing her forehead. 'Sophia, you have to listen to me. Andy is dangerous. He's not getting sued because he got on someone's bad side. He's getting trialled for aiding and abetting in the murder of three women and an attempt on a fourth. Sophia, *they* were pregnant, and he was the father.'

'I don't understand what you're saying,' Sophia said.

'How could you not?' Caitlyn said. 'Andy organised for those women to be dealt with, and no doubt he plans to do the same with you.'

Sophia's face paled and she slid down the door onto the ground, sitting with her knees bent and her head resting back against the door.

'Why would he do that?' she asked.

Caitlyn shook her head. 'I don't know,' she said. 'But I know that he could very well be capable of it. I never thought that he could hurt a fly, but he hurt me, Sophia. He found me in a friend's car the other night and he assaulted me.' She pointed to Sophia's wrists. 'And by the looks of it, he assaulted you, too.' Sophia started sobbing again. 'What did he say to you, Soph?'

She shook her head, the tears rolling down her cheeks. 'He wanted me to get rid of it,' she whispered. 'I thought he would be happy that he was going to be a father.'

'Sophia, you have to realise that you can't believe he won't do anything to you. He—' She paused, wondering how well Sophia would take the next bit. She was friends with Faith, but Sophia and Faith were near on inseparable, even before Caitlyn was friends with them. 'He was behind Faith's death. It wasn't entirely an accident.'

'No, the man who killed her already pleaded guilty,' Sophia said.

'Who do you think was behind it?' Caitlyn asked. 'Faith kept secrets, too. She'd been meeting up with Andy, and she got pregnant. You have to take the protective custody, Soph, please. I can't have anything happening to you.'

Sophia nodded, wiping her tears away again. 'I know,' she whispered. 'Caitlyn?'

'Yes?'

'Does this mean that you've forgiven me?'

Caitlyn paused, looking at Sophia, who looked so helpless, defenceless, but still hopeful. She shook her head. 'It's going to take me a long time to forgive you,' she said. 'But it's a start.'

Sophia rose to her feet, straightening herself, and started to walk to the next room. 'I understand,' she said. She ducked out of sight for a moment and returned with a travel bag. 'But maybe this would help.'

'You have my bag!' Caitlyn said, taking the bag from her, and searching through it. Clothes, her purse, her phone, her charger—it was all there. Everything she'd packed for her honeymoon was in the bag, which meant that she now had all of her belongings that were actually important to her.

'I hoped that I might have seen you again,' Sophia said. 'I figured you'd have to, since you'd eventually need everything in the bag.'

'Thank you,' Caitlyn said, smiling at Sophia, even though she hadn't thought it would be possible to even smile at her earlier. Maybe the bag would help her a little with the whole forgiving thing.

***

'So, do you feel relieved that Sophia accepted the protective custody?' Axel asked.

He assumed that Caitlyn's conversation with Sophia must have gone well enough, since she managed to convince her into accepting the protective custody. They'd taken Sophia to the police station before leaving so that she wouldn't be alone and her and Caitlyn seemed to at least be getting along. Though, he could still feel the tension in the car on their way to the police station.

'I'm just glad that she'll be safe now,' Caitlyn said, handing a cup of tea to him, and sitting on the couch next to him with hers in her hand. Flop settled down at her feet.

It had been a long day, and his eyelids were heavy. Cameron's private investigator had managed to find Jessie Turner in record time, saying that it was possibly the easiest thing he'd ever done. As it turned out, Jessie was back in town visiting her family, which was the first place he'd looked for her. It didn't take long for Cameron to contact her and convince her to come into the office the next day to give a statement. They were running out of time to gather enough information against Andy. With the hearing on Thursday, Jessie was their last chance of a solid argument. Otherwise, all they had was his ex-fiancée and a convicted criminal.

'Are you okay?' he asked. 'It must have been hard for you to talk to her.'

She pulled her legs up and tucked them underneath her, sitting on them like a child, and stared into her cup. 'It was,' she said. 'But I'm okay. I didn't have much of a choice.'

'I'm sorry,' he said, stretching his arm across the back of the seat. He let his finger trace circles on her shoulder, even though he knew he shouldn't. 'It'll be over soon.'

'That's if they find him guilty,' she said solemnly.

'They will,' he said.

'What makes you so sure?' She finally glanced up at him.

He raised his eyebrows. 'Oh, ye of little faith,' he said, shaking his head. 'I know, because I'm going to make sure they do find him guilty.'

'I hope that's not being overconfident,' she teased, her lips turning into a smile.

'Is that so?' he said, shifting in his seat so that he was leaning closer to her. He brushed her fringe from her eyes. 'I wouldn't say I'm overconfident, but I am confident.'

He shouldn't be talking like this. He shouldn't have any hint of flirting in his tone. But he couldn't help it. He was feeling his resolve slip away quicker than he could retrieve it. He was exhausted, and he wasn't thinking straight. And he was sitting next to a beautiful woman with incredible eyes staring straight into his. He took her cup and put it on the coffee table with his, returning to exactly where he was a moment before.

'Why do I get the feeling we're not talking about the court case anymore?' she whispered, searching his eyes.

'Because I'm not talking about the court case,' he replied, his voice low, a rumble.

He brushed his thumb across her cheek, feeling the last of his resolve disappear as she closed her eyes and gently pressed her face against his hand. He moved his hand to the back of her neck and pulled her towards him, meeting her halfway, his lips on hers, gentle, unmoving. Since she got some of her things back from Sophia, she'd smelled of apple and cinnamon again, but now with the hint of vanilla she had in the morning. She was sexy—her smell, her taste, her looks, everything about her. And he wanted more.

He kissed her again, parting her lips with his, teasing them with the tip of his tongue until she opened her mouth enough for him to explore it. She was moving her mouth with his, pressing harder against him, wrapping her arms around his shoulders, and running her fingers through his hair. It felt good. It somehow felt … right.

Chapter 16

His mouth moved with hers. Every movement was reciprocated and met with the same force. He cupped her cheek with his free hand, his other hand still at the back of her neck and kissed her deeper. She could feel the butterflies flipping in her stomach, her thoughts scrambling, and something stirring. It was different to when he was sleep walking. She'd been surprised that night and everything was all so uncertain. But now ... it somehow felt right. Maybe she was fooling herself, caught up in the moment. It had been a big day for them both and she had found a strength she didn't know she'd had when she talked Sophia into getting protective custody.

She pulled him closer, feeling his hair move between her fingers as she moved her hand. She didn't care how wrong her mind was telling her that they were for each other. In that moment, they couldn't have been more right for each other, she was sure of it. She tried to ignore her thoughts, because even if they were still wrong for each other, she wanted him—she wanted everything that was him. And he obviously felt the same way.

He pulled his legs up onto the couch and moved onto his knees, his lips never leaving hers, his hands moving down her side to her hips. Slowly, she leaned back on the couch, his body following hers, until she was laying with him leaning over her. She could taste the sweetness of his tongue, tinged with copper, and the smell of his woody cologne sent her head spinning. Or maybe it was the hormones that sent her head spinning. She wasn't sure. But she was certain about one thing—she needed him.

They heard a knock at the door. She tried to move, but Axel didn't budge. He broke their kiss, only slightly, just enough to form coherent words.

'Ignore it,' he said, planting his lips back on hers.

And she tried to. After all, who could it be? She figured if it was Tash, she would probably just let herself in anyway. She relaxed again, revelling in his touch as he slid his hands under her shirt and moved them across her back. She would have forgotten that someone was at the door until they heard another knock.

'Hey, Bad Ax! I know you're in there!' the voice yelled.

Axel shot upright, looking over at the door, his face looking like he'd just seen a ghost. He climbed off the couch and walked slowly towards it, breathing deeply. He paused a few feet from the door as the knocking happened again.

'Everything okay?' Caitlyn whispered, sitting up and straightening her clothes.

He furrowed his brow, shrugging. 'There's only one person who has ever called me that,' he said.

***

And he, sure as hell, planned on never seeing him again. At least he didn't have to wait too long for his body to cool off, since being interrupted and having to see this guy again was a total mood kill.

'Come on, man! I know you live here. I bumped into Tash, and she said you'd be home!'

He took another breath and opened the door. 'Hey, Tony.'

'What's it been, like, eight years?' Tony said, stretching his arms out. 'I feel like I've aged just waiting for you to open the door.'

Eight years that still wasn't long enough. 'It's been a while,' he said, flatly. 'What are you doing here?'

'Is that any way to welcome an old friend?' Tony teased. 'I came to town with my girlfriend, doing the whole meeting the family thing. We just found out we'll have to stay for a few more days, so I figured we could catch up.'

Tony pushed past Axel into his house and started looking around. Catching up with Tony was the last thing Axel wanted to do—one he hadn't ever intended to do since cutting him out of his life.

'Tony, it's not really a good—'

'Oh, I hope I'm not interrupting anything,' Tony continued, eyeing Caitlyn. 'I didn't know your bachelor days are over, Bad Ax.'

'Like you said, it's been eight years,' Axel said. 'And Caitlyn is my, ahh, housemate.'

He saw Caitlyn drop her gaze out of the corner of his eye. He wondered if she was disappointed that he'd called her his housemate. But what else was he supposed to call her? The girl he lives with and can't seem to keep his hands off? They hadn't even talked about what they were, or what they would be apart from being housemates. He wasn't about to blurt anything out to Tony. The less he knew about Axel's life, the better. Not to mention that the bachelor days Tony was talking about were well and truly over.

'With benefits, I'm sure,' Tony said, turning towards Caitlyn, and leaning forward in a bow. 'A pleasure, milady.'

Caitlyn blushed. 'Actually, I just moved in,' she said, rising to her feet, and picking up her cup of tea. 'So, I'm going to go unpack and leave you two to catch up.'

Axel knew that she was just trying to get away from Tony. After all, it's not as though she really had anything to unpack. She'd already taken everything out of her one bag that she picked up from Sophia's and put it all away. It was obvious that she was feeling uncomfortable. Of course, he didn't want to have to expose her to all that was Tony. Then again, he didn't exactly want to accommodate for him, either. Tony waited until Caitlyn was out of sight and flopped onto the couch.

'So, you're tapping that? Nice.'

'Like I said,' Axel said. 'She's my housemate, not an object, with no benefits per se. Not that it would be any of your business anyway.'

'Seriously?' Tony said. 'The Bad Ax I know wouldn't be living with a pretty woman without getting any action. From memory, you were pretty smooth with the ladies.'

'Well, I've changed,' Axel said, shrugging. 'I guess you could say I grew up.'

'Sounds boring,' Tony said, leaning back on the couch, making himself at home.

Axel sat on the armchair and stared at Tony. He looked like he hadn't changed at all. His mannerisms and way of talking definitely hadn't.

'I'm just saying that, if I were you, I couldn't keep my hands off a pretty woman like her,' Tony continued.

'Unlike you, I have a bit of respect for women,' Axel said, his jaw clenched.

'Like I said, boring,' Tony said.

'How the hell are you even in a relationship?' Axel asked, finding it hard to believe that Tony could be so disrespectful and immature and still manage to find someone to be with.

'Unlucky,' Tony said, shrugging. 'Cupid shot his whole sheath of arrows at me.'

Axel couldn't believe it. Tony had no idea how lucky he actually was to fall in love. Honestly, Axel hadn't really been with anyone since the days when he and Tony were actually friends. He'd been on a few dates, but they never amounted to anything. Dealing with his stress and focussing on his career took precedence.

'So, I was thinking,' Tony said, sitting up and leaning his elbows on his knees. 'We should catch up for a few drinks. Does tomorrow sound good?'

Axel shook his head. 'I don't think so, man,' he said. 'I'm not into that scene anymore.'

'You expect me to believe that you don't drink anymore?' he asked. 'Come on, for old time's sake.'

'Believe what you want,' Axel said, shrugging. 'But I'm not. I can't believe you still do—you were there when it happened, too.'

Tony's face grew solemn. 'A few drinks aren't a bad thing, Ax,' he said. 'I find it even helps me deal with it.'

'Well, I don't,' Axel said.

'You can't really be still dwelling on it, are you?'

'You're not?' Axel retorted.

'No, I'm not,' Tony said, standing to his feet. 'I got over it.'

'It's not just something you *get over*, Tony,' Axel said, standing as well.

'Maybe not for you, but my girlfriend has helped me with it. Maybe you should try it with your *housemate*,' Tony said. 'Have you even bothered to see him after that night?'

Axel felt his jaw clench. This was why he'd cut Tony out of his life. Their friendship was unhealthy. Everything that their friendship revolved around was unhealthy. And now, they would forever have a wedge between them.

'I didn't think so,' Tony said.

'I think you should leave,' Axel replied.

'Already out the door,' Tony said, heading towards the door. 'You know, I tried, man. That's all in the past. So, if you find yourself ready for those drinks while I'm in town, give me a call.'

'I'm busy,' Axel said, flatly.

It wasn't entirely a lie, he would be busy. With the hearing the day after tomorrow, he was short on time. He was sure that he would have had time to catch up for a drink in the evening, but it really wasn't his scene anymore. Not after that night. He hadn't touched any kind of alcohol to his lips since then. He'd thought that Tony would have been the same. Obviously not.

'Whatever, man,' Tony said, leaving. 'I'll be seeing you.'

Or he won't, if Axel could help it.

***

Caitlyn heard the door close and emerged from her room, meeting Axel as he was about to head into his room.

'So, who was that?' she asked, leaning against her doorframe.

'Just someone I used to be friends with,' he replied.

'Used to?' Caitlyn said. 'What happened?'

Axel shrugged. 'It doesn't matter, it's history.'

'What did he want, then?'

'What is this, twenty questions?'

'I—' Caitlyn paused. She'd thought that he might have been teasing when he said that, but his eyes had that cold, hardened look in them. She swallowed. He had been so tender and warm right before Tony showed up. And now? Now, it was as though his tender side would seem to be non-existent if she didn't know it was there, somewhere. 'I heard him ask you to have some drinks with him. That sounds like he wants to mend whatever happened between you.'

'Well, you don't know Tony,' he said. 'Did you also hear me tell him that it's not happening?'

Caitlyn crossed her arms and shrugged. 'If you said no because of me, you shouldn't have,' she said. 'I wouldn't be offended. In fact, I think that having a few drinks with him might not be such a bad idea. What harm could it do?'

'For starters,' he said. 'Drinking can ruin someone's life.'

'It's only a few drinks,' she said.

'That's all it takes.'

'Well, my life has never been ruined by a few drinks,' she said. 'So, if you're worried it will wreck yours, you just have to know when to stop and be responsible.'

'I'm not talking about *my* life, Caitlyn,' he said, opening the door to his room. 'I made a decision to not drink. The least you could do is support that. And if you're smart, you wouldn't drink either.'

'Excuse me?'

'And what happened before we got interrupted,' he said, indicating towards the lounge room. 'It can't happen again.'

Axel closed the door before she could even think to say anything more. She went into her own room and shoved the door closed, sliding down the door to sit on the ground. What the hell happened there? Whoever this Tony was, he must have struck a nerve with Axel.

They'd felt a true connection—or what she thought was true—before Tony showed up. She didn't even know how they got to that point. One minute, they were talking about Sophia and the court case. The next, they were kissing so tenderly, so passionately, and it was very rapidly leading to something more. She supposed that it was probably a good thing that Tony came when he did. It stopped them from making a mistake, after all. But he seemed to really bring the worst out in Axel.

She hadn't known him for long, but in that time, she hadn't figured him as one to go off the rails like that. Of course, it was an eye-opener. There was so much that she didn't know about Axel, but there was something there between them that just couldn't be ignored—she'd tried. But maybe, what she didn't know about Axel was big enough to help her ignore that connection. After all, with chemistry as strong as *that*, there must be something in his past that he's hiding.

Who was this Tony? She'd heard him ask Axel to have drinks with him *for old time's sake*, which means that there was a time when Axel did drink. And she'd noticed Axel's demeanour change when he heard Tony's voice—he tensed up, and his eyes grew wide, losing the passion that they'd had only moments before. Had something happened with him and Tony to make Axel completely swear off drinking? But if Tony was involved, why hadn't he given it up, too? She figured that people do cope differently, but from what she could see, Tony didn't seem so affected.

Axel mentioned that drinking ruins lives—even a few drinks. But a few drinks with friends had always been her life. Any social that she went to always had alcohol being rotated around the room. It was natural for her, so of course she couldn't understand why he was so sensitive about it. He didn't strike her as an alcoholic. But then, he also said that he wasn't talking about his life. So, whose life was he talking about? She wanted him to talk with her, to explain what happened, not lose his nut at her. She knew nothing of Axel's past.

Really, she knew nothing about Axel. All she actually knew about him was where he worked, where he lived, that he had a sister, and the fact that he was a very good kisser. As in, incredibly good. But that wouldn't be enough for them to build any kind of relationship on, and certainly wasn't enough to build trust. She touched the tips of her fingers to her lips, still tingling from his kisses. They'd been so close to doing more and she wouldn't have objected. Those kisses, and the chemistry they had, it all felt so incredibly real. She'd never felt how she felt then when Andy had kissed her—and she'd done more with Andy which turned out to be an act. But, somehow, some part of her wanted to trust that her connection with Axel was real. The rest of her told her that it wasn't enough, and it could never be enough.

Chapter 17

He hated that Tony made him overreact. Caitlyn didn't deserve to be snapped at like he did last night. But maybe it was for the better. He couldn't let anything happen between them—it would just complicate things. He knew they wouldn't work and still he'd lost control again. Now that she was obviously annoyed at him for snapping at her, it might be easier to resist.

But it still wasn't like him to lose his temper like that, and certainly not at someone who didn't deserve it, and never at someone who didn't have anything to do with putting him in that mood. And Caitlyn had nothing to do with getting him in a foul mood. If anything, it was the opposite with her. She made him lose control and feel things he hadn't felt before—with anyone. She had a hold on him and part of him didn't want to let her go.

Thinking about it had kept him awake—again—and he would have apologised to her for snapping like that if she was also awake, but she was still in bed when he left. He thought about waking her and decided against it. He thought about sneaking another kiss while she slept, but he knew that would have been crossing the line. So, he left. Like he'd said to her last night, it couldn't happen again.

'Axel, are you in there?'

Axel snapped out of his thoughts, realising that he had been staring at the wall for the last however long and looked across the desk at Cameron. They had been waiting for Jessie Turner to come in to give her statement and were supposed to be planning their approach together, except that Axel hadn't heard anything that Cameron had been saying.

'Did you hear anything I said?' Cameron asked.

Axel shook his head. 'Sorry, man,' he said. 'Didn't get much sleep.'

'That's not going to do, Axel,' Cameron said. 'We need to be on the same page with this and she'll be here any minute. Now, there's no time to fill you in on it, again.'

'Well, maybe I'll let you take this one by yourself,' he said. 'And I'll make myself a coffee so that I have a chance of waking up for everything else we have to do today.'

'That sounds like a good idea,' Cameron said.

'Who arranges to give their statement so early in the morning anyway?'

'Someone who doesn't want to be seen coming into the office,' Cameron replied.

Axel left Cameron's office and headed to their little kitchen to make himself a coffee, hearing their office door open and Cameron speak.

'Miss Turner,' Cameron said. 'You can come right through.'

'I'll just wait for you here, babe,' a familiar voice said.

Axel heard the door to Cameron's office close and built up the courage to go to the couched waiting area—after all, he had been a bit harsh on Tony last night, too. Tony had said that he and his girlfriend had found out that they had to stay in town a little longer than they planned, but he'd never said what for. The fact that Tony was now sitting on a couch in his office waiting room explained why. And out of all the people that Tony could have fallen in love with, it sure struck Axel as interesting that he'd fallen in love with Jessie Turner.

'Well, this explains why you had to stay in town,' Axel said, leaning on the door frame.

Tony's eyes shot up towards Axel like a stunned rabbit. 'What are you doing here?'

Axel shrugged. 'I work here,' he said, pointing to his name on the door next to him.

'So much for coming early so we wouldn't see anyone we knew,' Tony said, staring at his hands. 'So, a lawyer, huh? That was probably at the bottom of the list of careers I thought you might have.'

Axel smiled. 'What was at the top?'

Tony looked up, a smile tugging at his lips. 'A gigolo.'

'Seriously?' Axel asked, laughing.

'Like I said, you always had a way with the ladies,' Tony teased. 'But seriously, I never figured you for one to have a career where you have to focus more on your job than your women.'

'And like I said,' Axel said, taking a seat opposite Tony. 'I've changed. That hasn't been my world since our gap year days.'

'So, why a lawyer?' Tony asked.

'Figured it would keep me out of trouble,' Axel said.

'Has it worked?'

'Up until recently,' Axel replied.

'Your housemate?' Tony asked. Axel nodded. 'I get it. I thought I was doing all right until I met Jessie. Then I realised how little I was coping. She really did help, you know? But now this ...' He paused, looking back at his hands and shaking his head. 'I had no idea about her history until now. The stuff she's been through—it just makes me feel like what we went through was nothing.'

'It wasn't nothing,' Axel said. 'It's just a different kind of something.'

'Still,' Tony said. 'You can see why she doesn't want to be anywhere near that bastard. Do you think a recorded testimony would suffice?'

'I don't think Andy Graeme even knows that she's still alive,' Axel said. 'So, it's probably best that we keep her away from him, anyway.'

'It'll be good when it's all over,' Tony said. 'And we can get out of this town again. Maybe with it all of it behind us, she'll finally agree to marry me.'

'Marry you?' Axel asked. 'You really are settling down.'

Tony shrugged. 'Like I said, I got attacked by Cupid.'

Axel smiled. Obviously, he wasn't the only one who had changed over the years after all. 'Tony, I think I might have been a bit harsh on you last night,' he said. 'I mean, I really don't drink anymore, but that doesn't mean we can't catch up. It has been eight years, after all.'

'It's all good, man,' Tony said. 'To be honest, I haven't really enjoyed it since, anyway. I don't know why I thought of it. Old habits, I guess.'

'I haven't visited him,' Axel said after a moment of silence, staring at the floor. 'Dante. I haven't seen him since I saw you last. Have you seen him at all?'

Tony nodded. 'I kept visiting him for a while,' he said. 'Every week for a few months. But we never talked about much. Dante always talked about you, asking if I'd seen you, if I'd heard from you, if you planned on coming to see him. It never changed. He always asked about you and I could never tell him what he wanted to hear. So, I stopped visiting him.'

'I didn't know,' Axel said.

'You didn't care,' Tony said.

'That's not true,' Axel said. 'I wanted to, I just—'

'You don't need to make up excuses to me,' Tony said, waving his hand at Axel. 'Dante's the one who wanted to see you.'

'I should have visited,' Axel said solemnly.

'You should have,' Tony said. 'But you didn't.'

'I couldn't.'

Axel couldn't have been saying anything truer. He couldn't see Dante. He couldn't face him after what happened. And he'd tried so hard to distract himself enough to forget his past, but it still flared up in his dreams. He could never forget it. He'd tried, and he'd never succeeded. He never would.

'I have to ask you something,' Tony said, breaking the silence. Axel looked up at him. 'Did I actually interrupt something when I came over last night?'

Axel tried to suppress a smile. 'You know I don't kiss and tell.'

'Bad Ax, you sly dog,' Tony said, breaking into a toothy grin. 'Still living up to your nickname.'

Axel laughed. 'It's just as well you interrupted, anyway,' he said, looking back down at the floor. 'It could never work.'

'When has that ever bothered you?'

'When it could actually mean something,' Axel said, frowning.

'So, why can't it work?' Tony asked.

Axel shrugged. 'We're from two different worlds,' he started.

'She's living with you, isn't she?' Tony asked. Axel nodded. 'Doesn't sound like it's that different to me.'

'It's temporary,' Axel said, convinced that it truly was.

'What if it's not?'

Axel looked up at Tony. Once upon a time, he would never have taken any advice from him—especially relationship advice. But here he was, the one with an almost-fiancée, clearly happier than Axel had ever been, asking him a very valid question. What if it's not?

***

She shouldn't be worrying about frivolous things. Axel obviously regretted what happened between them—he made that clear last night. But then, he took another step to confuse her. She'd heard him knock quietly on her door before going to work this morning. She'd heard him nudge open the door to look in and whispered her name. And she'd kept her eyes closed and lay as still as she possibly could, hoping that he thought she was still asleep. Her feelings were so over the place that she couldn't tell if she was mad at him, upset that he didn't want anything more, relieved because things with him would just be complicated, or so desperate for his touch that it consumed her every thought. Whatever it was, he was always there in her mind, and it was driving her crazy.

So, of course, the only thing she could think of, after surviving a rollercoaster of emotions all night, was to lay as still as she possibly could. Maybe after the hearing tomorrow, her thoughts might realign themselves to where they're supposed to be, and she could get some order back in her life. For now, she had to do her best to create the order with what she had. And she felt like she was failing miserably.

She drooped her head over the edge of the couch, her legs raised over the back of it, and covered her face with her hands. God, if she could just get Axel out of her head and only look at him as her housemate—a friend—then it would make her life so much easier. But for some reason, she couldn't look at him as just a friend. A woman can't be just friends with someone who she has an undeniable attraction to. And she was sure that attraction was mutual. Why else would he have kissed her?

She knew that he struggled with stress. Could that make him do things he didn't really want to do? But his kisses seemed so deliberate and she could tell that he'd wanted it. And if Tony hadn't interrupted them, she was certain that they would have deliberately done more and neither of them would have stopped it. But would that have made him regret it more? She wasn't even sure if she regretted it. As far as she was concerned, she wished that they hadn't kissed like that—only because it made her want more. She just wished that they didn't have to try to forget the chemistry between them because it could never work. After all, how would they know it wouldn't work without first giving it a go?

Axel had eased himself into her life and she couldn't stop him, nor did she want to. And she would be willing to take the risk, to see where things lead with him. They might fight and fall apart quicker than she could realise what was happening, or they might work out—at least they would know. But now, there was the one thing that was truly coming between them, and that was whatever happened between him and Tony because it was obviously something that affected him.

She heard the front door jar open and jolted upright. Axel should be home by now and she didn't want him seeing her in such an unladylike position.

'Is it safe to come in?'

She slumped back on the couch, but kept her feet on the ground this time.

'It's just me, Tash,' she said.

Tash poked her head around the door and opened it wide, satisfied that she wasn't intruding on anything.

'Axel's not home?' she asked. Caitlyn shook her head. 'I thought he might have been.'

'I guess he's still sorting everything out for the hearing tomorrow,' Caitlyn said. 'Were you hoping to talk to him?'

Tash shook her head. 'I'm looking for my sandals,' she said, busying herself with looking under everything. 'I forgot to grab them the other day.' She pulled out her sandals from under a box and held them up. 'Here they are,' she said. 'How are you feeling about the hearing, anyway?'

'Nervous, to say the least,' Caitlyn said. 'More like freaking out.'

'You'll be fine,' Tash said. 'Has Axel gone through it all with you yet?'

Caitlyn shook her head. 'I'm sure he would have last night,' she said, not entirely convinced herself. 'But we kind of got … interrupted.'

Tash raised an eyebrow. 'Do I want to know why?'

Caitlyn laughed. 'Not like that.' Although it almost was. 'Tony dropped by.'

'Tony?' Tash's eyes widened. 'As in Tony who Axel hasn't talked to in eight years Tony?'

Caitlyn nodded. 'That's what I gathered.'

'I didn't know he was in town,' Tash said.

'Are you sure?' Caitlyn asked. Tash nodded. 'He said that he'd bumped into you and you said that Axel would be home.'

'Caitlyn, *I* haven't seen Tony in eight years,' Tash said. 'I don't know how he found out where Axel lives or that he was even home, but it wasn't from me.'

'So, he was—'

'Lying,' Tash finished. 'But it probably doesn't really matter. How did Axel take his visit, anyway?'

'Terribly,' Caitlyn said. 'He practically kicked him out.'

'Doesn't surprise me,' Tash said.

'Tash, what happened between them?' Caitlyn asked.

'It's not my place to say,' Tash said, looking down at her watch. 'You'll have to ask Axel. I have to go now, anyway. Liam's waiting for me.'

Caitlyn watched as Tash left, feeling even more nervous about the hearing than she did before. Where was Axel? If he'd come home when he should have so that they could practice, maybe she wouldn't be so nervous. Tomorrow, Andy could be found guilty and she wouldn't have to worry about seeing him again. Or, he could be deemed innocent and she wouldn't be able to stay here—not if she's testifying against him. Not with how he assaulted her the other night, and assaulted Sophia afterwards. She knew what Andy could be capable of, and she didn't want to be on the receiving end of it.

Chapter 18

Axel stopped pacing and looked her straight in the eye. She had to get this right—she had to be convincing enough to convince the jury that Andy was guilty, or at least enough to make them question his innocence. Caitlyn had her focus on him.

'Miss Low,' he started. 'Why did you leave Andy Graeme at the altar?'

Her eyes glinted. 'Because he's a bastard.'

'Caitlyn!' He sat down on the chair opposite her, dropping his head into his hands. 'Do you realise how convincing you have to be? The jury can't have any doubt about your testimony.'

Caitlyn threw her head back against the couch. 'Come on, Axel,' she said. 'We've been rehearsing this for hours. Can't we call it quits for the night? I'm sure I could do a good enough job of convincing them.'

'It has to be second nature to you, Caitlyn,' he said. 'Your statement has to be exactly the same every time you say it—there can't be any discrepancy with it.'

'It's not like I'm making it up, Axel,' she said. 'He *did* get my best friend pregnant while we were together, and he *did* assault me, and he *did* tell Sophia to have an abortion.'

'I know,' Axel said. 'It's just that we have to convince the jury and the judge that he is capable of doing what we're trying to prove he did.'

'I'm not the only one testifying,' Caitlyn said.

'Yes, but you'll be the one asked the most targeted questions since you were with the guy for eight years,' he said. 'Which is why you have to be the most convincing, Caitlyn.'

'The most convincing?' she asked. 'Why do you say it as if my life depends on it?'

'Because it could,' he said. He dropped to his knees in front of her, taking her hands in his. 'Caitlyn, you were with him for *eight years.*'

'You already said that,' she whispered, looking into his eyes.

'No doubt, there will be some jury members who will question whether you had anything to do with it,' he said, swallowing.

'Why would they think that?'

'Think about it Caitlyn,' he said, extending his arms out. 'How do they know that you didn't initiate the order to have the girls taken care of?'

'What?'

She looked like she'd just been slapped, but he had to keep going. He had to make sure she knew that questioning can get intense in court, that the blame can sometimes be shifted to one of the witnesses.

'You had reason to—you were in a relationship with him.'

'Axel,' she said, her eyes widening.

He shrugged. 'You could have given him an ultimatum, pulled the strings, making sure the girls were dealt with and taken out of the picture.'

'I couldn't,' she said.

'How do I know you're not lying?' he asked, sitting back on the chair, his voice raised a little louder.

'Because I didn't do it!'

'That's not good enough, Caitlyn!' he yelled. Her eyes were glistening, but he couldn't stop. She had to be pushed to the breaking point.

'I left him for cheating on me,' she yelled back. 'Why the hell wouldn't I have left him the first time he cheated on me?'

'You tell me.'

'I didn't even *love* him!' The tears were steadily rolling down her cheeks now. 'I didn't love him, Axel. I was waiting for an excuse good enough to justify leaving him. God, if I knew—' She broke off and wiped her eyes. 'If I knew what he'd done, I would have left him years ago and maybe,' she continued, lowering her voice and looking up at him. 'Maybe those girls would still be alive. Faith was my friend and I was devastated to hear that she'd died. I didn't even know that she was pregnant.'

Axel stared at her for a moment, her eyes unmoving. She didn't love him. She'd been with the guy for eight years, and she didn't love him. 'Good,' he said, standing up and picking up their cups to take to the sink. 'Now we can call it a night.'

'Good?' Caitlyn said, shaking her head. 'Wait—'

'I will try my best to keep any questioning off that nature, but sometimes the defending lawyers play dirty, Caitlyn,' he continued. 'You need to be prepared for it if they do. You had me convinced, so I have no doubt you'll be able to convince them.'

She jumped to her feet and followed him to the kitchen, stomping her feet. 'You played me!' she said.

'Yes, I did,' he said, putting the cups down. 'And you did well.'

'Thank you,' she said.

He turned to face her, her eyes catching him by surprise. He'd expected her eyes to be cold, angry because he'd played her like that. But they were warm, and dancing, and a smile tugged at her lips. She inched her body closer to him, tilting her shoulder in a flirtatious manner, biting her bottom lip. She'd had him pressed against the kitchen bench, moving her head closer to his, not taking her eyes off his. Her eyes were inviting, seductive, and her lips were only an inch away from his. He nudged his mouth closer to close the gap and she pulled away.

'We need to talk,' she said, moving her body away from him.

Shoot. The damn minx could play him, too.

***

'And what do we need to talk about?' he asked, his voice teasing.

She knew that she probably shouldn't have flirted with him like that. It was, after all, a very different kind of playing to what he was doing. And she had almost lost it. He was way too tempting for that kind of play, and if she didn't feel the desperate need to talk to him about what happened last night, she wouldn't have had anything to stop her. The truth was, she was thankful that he'd pushed her like that. Even if it wasn't brought up in her questioning, he had pushed her to the point of realising that she'd never loved Andy. The whole time they had been together—she had never loved him. She never really knew what love was, and she still didn't.

But what she felt with Axel excited her. It's as though he'd stirred in her something that she never knew was there. She had accepted what she had with Andy as the normal—as the best it could be. But now, she knew better. With everything that Axel made her feel in the last week since the whole coffee incident, she knew that there was so much more to it than she had ever thought. And somehow, she could tell that what she felt with Axel was just the beginning.

There was only one thing that was stopping her from letting go and letting herself explore things with Axel, and that was Andy. If things went wrong with the hearing tomorrow, she would have no choice but to leave. She wouldn't know for certain, but she was sure he wouldn't be happy about her testifying against him in court. And if that was the case, she probably wouldn't be much better off than the women before her. And if she had to leave, she would be leaving Axel behind.

So, of course, she knew how much was relying on her statement being convincing. The last thing she wanted to do was uproot what little of her life she had left and go on the run for the rest of her life, seeing Andy Graeme as the Mayor of Goulburn and the man who essentially got away with murder in the papers and on the news living his life with complete freedom.

'Caitlyn?'

She looked up at Axel and realised that she hadn't answered his question yet. 'Last night,' she said hesitantly. 'We have to talk about it.'

He shrugged, though his demeanour didn't change like it had the night before. 'There's nothing to talk about,' he said simply.

'But we—' she started. 'That wasn't nothing.'

'No, it wasn't,' he said, brushing her fringe away from her eyes. 'We kissed, Caitlyn, and we got interrupted. That's all it was.'

'Was it?' she asked.

'What?'

'A kiss,' she said. 'Was that really all it was? Because I've been kissed before, and that wasn't just a kiss.' He clenched his jaw, as if trying to stop himself from saying something, from doing something. 'Axel, talk to me,' she continued. 'Was that really just a kiss for you?' She held her breath, waiting for him to answer.

'Caitlyn,' he said, searching her eyes with his. 'I'd be lying if I said that there was nothing else there, or that I didn't want more and that I didn't find you hard to resist. But we can't. Not with everything that's going on right now.'

She exhaled, or rather, she felt as though she'd been punched in the chest, knocking the wind right out of her. 'Why not?' she breathed.

His brow furrowed. 'You already know the answer to that,' he whispered back.

She nodded, because she did know why they couldn't be together. And she wished that their circumstances could be different, but then, if they were, perhaps they would never have met. And perhaps she wouldn't be standing here now, staring into his gorgeous steel-grey eyes, and feeling more raw and vulnerable than she had ever thought possible and had ever felt before. And maybe, her desires wouldn't get the better of her, knowing that she could lose everything tomorrow.

'But what if we could?' she whispered.

'Caitlyn,' he said, a hint of warning in his voice.

'Axel, please,' she said. 'We both want it. So, what's really stopping us?'

She reached down for his hand and tangled her fingers between his, feeling the perfect fit of their hands. He rested his forehead against hers, his eyes closed, shaking his head slowly from side to side.

'You shouldn't tempt me,' he said.

'I'm asking you,' she whispered.

He opened his eyes, looking into hers, his eyes wild, and let go of her hand, wrapping both of his arms around her and pressing his lips against hers. She wrapped her arms around the back of his neck and let him pull her body against his, deepening the kiss. She could taste the sweet copper of his lips and felt the stirring inside her stomach. He excited her. And she craved more of him.

She parted her lips, letting him explore her mouth with his tongue and teased him back with hers. He moved his hands down her back, stopping at her hips and pulling her harder against him, even though she thought that the only way their bodies could be closer is if they'd had no clothes on at all. He moved his hands to the top of her thighs, just below her bottom, and picked her up, his lips still on hers, sitting her on the kitchen bench. She slid closer to him, wrapping her legs around his waist as he moved his hands up her side, slowly pulling her shirt up over her head, breaking the kiss only to let the shirt pass.

She could feel the trail of fire that his fingers left everywhere they touched, her body tingling in anticipation of more. She tilted her head to the side as he moved his mouth down her neck and across her collarbone, nipping and kissing every inch while she worked on his shirt buttons, one at a time, pushing his shirt off his shoulders and gripping her fingers around his muscles. He moved his mouth back over where he'd been kissing, hovering only slightly above her skin and met her lips with his again, kissing her tenderly, passionately, pressing his naked chest against her.

It felt as though there was no time, that any minute or second stood still for them as they kissed. She could feel the heat of his body radiating against hers and she was filled with want and pure desire. She ran her hands through his hair, feeling the softness travel between her fingers, and broke the kiss, her lips only an inch away from his.

'Axel,' she pleaded.

'Hold on,' he said, pulling her mouth back to his.

She tightened her legs around his hips and he cupped his hands on her bottom, pulling her as close to him as she could get and lifted her up, carrying her towards his bedroom. Their lips didn't part until he'd laid her on his bed and he left a trail of kisses down the front of her neck, down to the mounds of her breasts. He slid his hands underneath her back, unclipping her bra, and moving it to the side, pushing it onto the ground, and cupped her breasts with his hands.

This was it. This was her, raw and vulnerable, and the man who she found irresistible.

***

She was perfect, stunning. Everything about her sent him wild with desire. She met his every kiss with the same passion as his, and everywhere his mouth touched on her soft skin pushed him closer to the edge. He needed her, and he needed her now. He could see the glow of her body in the soft moonlight beaming through his window.

'God, you are beautiful,' he said, wondering if he'd imagined the darker tinge in her cheeks.

He started kissing her neck again, giving her body the attention it deserved. He couldn't believe that a woman like her would even consider anything with a broken man like him, but then, she didn't know how broken he was. He moved his mouth over the peaks of her breasts and teased her with his tongue. He could feel her arching her body against him as he teased her other side with his fingertips. She let out a soft moan as he swapped sides, licking and sucking, then moved his lips down her stomach until he got to the top of her pants. He tugged at her pants slowly, soaking up every little bit of her bare skin with his gaze and kissing the tender points where her hips met her thighs. With every inch of skin he uncovered as he moved her pants and undies down, he left a trail of kisses.

Once her pants were off, he slid his hands up the inside of her legs until he felt the warmth and moistness of her wanting. She moaned again as he moved his fingers and it pushed him closer and closer to losing control.

'Axel, please,' she begged.

And that was what pushed him beyond all control. His pants were off before he could even think about it, and he was hovering a breath above her, savouring all that was her.

'Please don't make me beg,' she whispered.

'Maybe I want you to,' he teased.

She pulled him closer and kissed him passionately, wrapping her legs around his waist, pressing his body closer to her with her feet until he was as deep as he could go. He was wild for her, and she was frantic for him, kissing passionately, ferociously, and moving rhythmically as one. And he knew that she would never have to beg for more.

Chapter 19

For the first time all week, Caitlyn had finally managed to get a good night's sleep. Well, it was the most enjoyable, at least, even though there wasn't much sleep involved. She'd thought that, if they caved just the once, maybe it would help them resist each other. But she was a fool for thinking that. And the fact that they'd made love twice more after that first time proved the point. And the fact that she could barely keep her eyes off him all morning simply showed her that she would have one hell of a time forgetting him if things went wrong.

So, she sat there, her eyes on Axel, amazed at how good he was at his job and praying to God that Andy Graeme would be sent to jail and she could live her life—hopefully with Axel in the picture. The wait for the jury to come back out to give their verdict seemed like it lasted forever. The courtroom was silent for the most part. She guessed there was a lot riding on it. Or that she was too caught up in her thoughts to notice any conversation that could have been happening.

She stared at the back of Axel, taking in his neat hair and his broad shoulders framed by his suit and smiled at the memory of his muscles as she ran her hands over them the night before. She could still feel his kisses and his touch all over her body and it sent her stomach flipping. She'd caught him a few times, glancing in her direction out of the corner of his eye while they waited, and she'd thought that she saw him flash a quick smile at her. But she could have been mistaken. After all, the morning was strictly business.

She'd testified against Andy Graeme, and she'd watched as others did the same and Cameron and Axel presented evidence against him. She'd observed the expressions of the jury members and hoped that she'd read them right. She was convinced that Andy Graeme was guilty, and she'd thought it would be an easy decision for the jury members. But they were taking their time, and that made her nervous. Every minute seemed like an hour, and she wondered if Axel felt the same anxiety that she was feeling now.

He didn't look like it. He looked relaxed, professional. She wondered if it always took this long to wait for the jury to come to a decision. But then, she supposed, not every case would be trialling a public figure for being associated with murder on multiple accounts. Andy's involvement with those women and their fates still came as a shock to her. She felt like she'd just about dodged a bullet with him—but it wasn't over yet.

The room went silent as the jury members started to file through the door and back to their seats, the judge banging his hammer and focussing on the jury members.

'Has the jury come to a unanimous decision?' the judge asked.

'We have,' the spokesman said.

The slip of paper that the spokesman held was brought to the judge. She felt her breath catch in her throat as she watched the judge read the verdict. This was it—the decision that could change her life in any direction, and she wished that the judge would hurry it along before she passed out from not breathing. Finally, the judge leaned forward to speak into the microphone.

'The jury has found the defendant *guilty* of these charges,' he said. 'Mr Graeme, you will be held under police custody until the time of your sentencing. Court is adjourned.'

Guilty. Andy Graeme was guilty. Which she was already convinced that he was. So, why did it come as a shock to her now that the verdict was in? She glanced over at Axel again, hoping to catch his eye, but he was shaking hands with the defending lawyer.

She wouldn't have to leave town. She wouldn't have to uproot what's left of her life and be on the run. Andy Graeme was going to jail. And Axel is the one who put him there.

***

'Well, that must be the biggest case we've done lately,' Cameron said, shaking Axel's hand. 'Good work.'

'You're the one who did all the hard work,' Axel said back.

'Maybe so,' Cameron said. 'But you're the one that convinced the jury. I could see it in their faces.' He leaned in towards Axel, lowering his voice. 'Now, you can enjoy the girl.'

Axel's eyes widened as Cameron left to talk to Colin Jefferson. Had it been that obvious? Sure, he hadn't been able to get her out of his head, which he hadn't actually been able to do all week. But now, he'd had the added images of her naked body, the feel of her skin on his, and the softness of her lips as they kissed to think about. God, it had been so hard for him to keep a poker face as he questioned her. He hated having to do it, but he knew that she would be most comfortable and convincing if he was the one doing the questioning instead of Cameron.

And she hadn't faltered. Everything went exactly as rehearsed, and the defending lawyer didn't even have the guts to play dirty. She wasn't queried about whether she was involved with it. He supposed it was because Cameron had managed to get Sophia to testify as well. And now, it was over. Andy Graeme was going behind bars. He'd have no chance of ever becoming the Mayor of Goulburn. And Faith's memory, as well as the other women, could be honoured. He had promised Caitlyn that he would make sure Andy Graeme was found guilty, and, for the most part, he had kept that promise.

He glanced over at Caitlyn—not for the first time during the hearing—and felt his insides stir to see how beautiful she was. But she didn't look as ecstatic about Andy being convicted than he thought she would be. Surely, she must be relieved, happy even, but he wasn't expecting her to look shocked. Without a second to change his mind, he moved towards her, being cut off before he could even reach the half-way point.

'Axel,' Tony said, reaching his hand out to shake hands with him.

Axel shook it. 'Tony, I didn't see you,' he said. 'Have you been here the whole time?'

Tony nodded. 'I've been up the back.'

'Jessie isn't here?' Axel asked, looking around the room.

'She didn't want him to see her,' he replied. 'She went through a lot, you know. I think she's still recovering from what he put her through.'

'Understandable,' Axel said. 'Well, she doesn't have to worry about him now. Justice has been served.'

'All thanks to you,' Tony said. 'I really can't thank you enough, man. I know it's your job and all, but it means that Jessie and I can get on with our lives. So, thank you.'

'Not a problem,' Axel said, patting Tony on the back. 'I have some things I have to do now,' he continued. 'Are you hanging around town or are you headed home?'

'Headed home,' he said. 'But I'm sure we'll be back more often now that we won't have to worry about that bastard anymore. Maybe we can catch up properly next time I'm in town.'

'Definitely,' Axel said, starting to move towards Caitlyn again before stopping. 'Tony?' Tony looked questioningly at him. 'It really is good to see you again. And I'm happy for you.'

'Thanks man,' Tony said, tapping the side of his pointer finger to his forehead. 'You, too.'

And he meant what he said. He had overreacted when Tony showed up at his door a couple of nights ago. He had been stressed with the whole hearing thing, and Caitlyn, of course. But now, he'd felt somewhat relieved. The case was over—well, for him anyway. Andy Graeme still had to have his sentence issued before he moved into his new home behind bars where he wouldn't be able to touch Caitlyn. She was safe. And that was all that mattered to him right now. And maybe, what happened between him and Caitlyn could be more than just a one-night thing. What could come between them now? He sat in the seat next to Caitlyn, trying to act as professional as he could since he shouldn't really be seen flirting with one of the witnesses.

'How are you holding up?' he asked. 'I thought you would be happy.'

'I am happy,' she said, unconvincingly. 'I think it's just all catching up with me.' She looked up at him, her eyes glistening, and he could feel his professionalism slipping away. 'You were amazing, by the way.'

He smiled, resisting the urge to tuck her hair behind her ears. 'I was just doing my job,' he said, coyly. 'And keeping a promise I made to a beautiful woman.'

Her cheeks tinged pink. 'I suppose a thank you is in order,' she said, a smile teasing her lips. 'Or do I congratulate you? I'm not really familiar with the post-hearing conversations.'

He shrugged. 'Both, I guess,' he said. 'What are you going to do now, Caitlyn?'

She shook her head. 'I don't know,' she said. 'I haven't really thought about it. I mean, I figured I'd have to run for the hills if he was found not guilty.'

'But you don't have to run, now.'

'No, I don't,' she said, staring at her hands.

'You could always stay,' he said, nudging her knee with his. 'With me. For a while, if you like. Or as long as you want.'

'That's really sweet of you, Axel,' she said, looking up at him again. He could feel everyone around him phasing out. He felt as though they were the only people in the room. 'But, I—'

'You don't have to decide right now,' he said, touching her hand briefly before remembering that he was supposed to act professional. 'But I would like to take you out for a celebratory dinner tonight.'

'As in, a date?'

He shrugged. 'Something like that.'

'And where will we go?' she asked, a flirtatious tone in her voice.

'I was thinking we could make a night of it,' he teased. 'We could dress up and follow our nose, see where it leads us.'

She bit her lip. 'I think I would like that,' she said.

He couldn't hold back the smile. 'Good.'

Chapter 20

'Ready to go?' Axel called.

Caitlyn took one last look in the mirror and tugged at the dress she borrowed from Tash. It was a little bit on the skimpy side for what she would usually wear, but she didn't have much of a choice. She had a feeling that Tash thought it would be funny to bring over her skimpiest black dress for Caitlyn to wear on her date with Axel. After all, it seemed that Tash was all for them starting something.

She thought about what Axel had said earlier about what she was going to do now that the hearing was over and how he had offered for her to stay. Had he really meant that? Or had he felt obliged to say it? On one hand, she hoped that he really did mean it and she wanted to. She would love to stay living with him, enjoying each other like they did last night. But she knew that it was only ever supposed to be temporary, and she was sure that he knew that, too. And sure, now she didn't have to leave.

But it also meant that, since the hearing was over, they had to find some more common ground to build on. Before now, it was the court case. It was a common ground that they could both relate to because, in one way or another, it affected them both. But now? Their only real common ground was their place of residence. So, that was her aim with this date. Sure, she knew that they worked well together in bed—at least, they did in the hype of the moment. But they hadn't really talked about much else other than the court case, and now that that was over, she was starting to realise how much she didn't know about Axel.

He was a mystery to her. All that she did know about him were mysteries—there were parts missing. The whole thing with Tony, why he has to take anti-depressants to help him deal with stress, what made him want to be a lawyer, his childhood and history in general. They were all mysteries, and ones that she'd love to know the answer to. And maybe he would fill in the gaps for her. Or maybe they were topics that were just too sensitive for him to talk about. She wondered if they would still have connected if they hadn't been focussing on the court case the whole time.

'Caitlyn?'

She let out a sigh, figuring that this would be the decisive moment. Hopefully, the night could go well, and she would have some clarity about what she might do from here. Otherwise, she would still be at a loss as to where her life was going to take her. She tugged the dress down a little to show a bit more cleavage, wondering if it would help with conversation, then pulled it back up, deciding that she wanted him to know the real her. After all, she didn't want to come across as a floozy by having everything hanging out for all to see. She had to leave some things up to the imagination. She felt a blush cross her cheeks. Yes, Axel would probably have a good imagination about what was underneath her clothes, considering he'd spent so much time giving every inch of her his undivided attention last night.

'I'm ready,' she said, opening her bedroom door, and stepping out, surprised to find him standing right there, almost bumping into him.

He smiled coyly. 'Oh, good,' he said. 'I was starting to think I might have to come in there and help you.'

'I'm sure you would have liked that,' she teased.

He reached out and tucked a stray hair behind her ear. 'I don't think I would have been much help getting you dressed, to be honest,' he said, his voice deep, husky, and sending a shiver down her spine. He ran his fingers down her arm. 'You look beautiful, by the way,' he added, leaning in to give her a kiss.

Without thinking, she turned her head slightly and pressed her cheek to his lips quickly. 'Are we off?' she asked, moving towards the door. She felt her heart drop quicker than a rock thrown off a cliff as she moved, regretting that she had potentially missed one last kiss with him and feeling like a terrible person for cheeking the person she'd slept with the night before.

'Sure,' he said.

She closed her eyes briefly before opening the front door. She was sure that she could sense some coldness in his voice. And she didn't blame him.

***

He hadn't expected her to cheek him. Not now. Not at the start of their first proper date. Not after the night they had. And not after having won the case today. Sure, he was nervous. And he was sure that she was too, especially with how long she took to get ready for their date. Not that he was complaining about how long she took, since he wanted to rip her dress off her the second he laid eyes on her. He thought that she would have appreciated his compliment, or at least be looking forward to going on their date. But now, he wasn't so sure.

He wondered what she must be thinking. If he had this much going through his head, surely she had about a million more things that would make it hard to focus on anything. It may have been a while since he'd been on a date, but he was pretty sure that he wasn't usually the factor in the terrible dates he'd had previously. And with the terrible dates that he had been on, there was never any chemistry between them—certainly not like there was with Caitlyn. He and Caitlyn had that irresistible, impossible to forget, and even harder to resist kind of chemistry. Or, at least, he thought they did. Right now, no one would be able to guess that they'd ever had any kind of connection.

They kept walking, a good metre between them. To start the date, he'd tried to hold her hand, but she'd crossed her arms instead, commenting about everywhere looking busy tonight. He couldn't work out where it all went wrong. Sure, their relationship had been sort of backwards and all over the place, considering she moved in with him before sleeping with him, and all of that was before they'd even been on a date.

Last night had been her idea, after all. He was planning to at least take her on a date after the court case before pursuing more with her. But how could he say no to her when she'd practically begged him for one night? He'd wanted it from the second he first laid eyes on her and had struggled to keep his hands off her since. So, of course, her asking him for it just made him lose the little bit of self-control that he did have. And he was sure that she had enjoyed it—he knew he did—especially since she'd wanted it again. And again! So, why was she so distant now? And why couldn't they keep a conversation going?

'Has anything caught your nose, yet?' he asked.

'What?' she asked, glancing up at him briefly before returning her stare to the ground in front of them.

'Well, since we're trying to decide where to go for dinner by seeing what smell draws us in,' he explained, not for the first time tonight. 'Has anything caught your nose?'

'Oh,' she said. 'No.'

He didn't even know what to say to that, so he kept quiet, nodding his head, and kept walking, quickening their pace a little. If they weren't going to decide on anywhere to eat, then they may as well get the walking part of it over with.

'You should have made a reservation somewhere,' she mumbled.

'I figured this would be more fun,' he said. 'Since I didn't want to make a reservation somewhere that you hate.'

'And how is that working out for you?'

He turned to face her, stopping in his tracks, grabbing hold of her arm. 'What do you want from me, Caitlyn?' he asked, spreading his arms out. 'I'm trying, here.'

'Are you?' she retorted, coldly.

He felt his body jolt a little. 'What's that supposed to mean?' he asked through his teeth.

She shrugged. 'Well, for starters, you don't even have an idea in your mind of where you're taking me,' she said. 'We've been walking up and down the street for the last hour and a half and, so far, we haven't set foot into a restaurant.'

'It's not like I had a long time to plan an elaborate date,' he said.

She let out a laugh, making him clench his jaw more than it already was. 'You can't seriously be telling me that you had no idea where we would eat when you asked me out,' she said, shaking her head.

'Following our nose *was* the plan,' he said.

'And it's not working,' she said, starting to walk again.

'Well, I'm sorry I don't live up to your expectations,' he said sarcastically. 'What do you expect, Caitlyn? I'm not uptight and structured. In fact, I have no structure in my life, at all. I never had. I'm not rich or running for Mayor like Andy was.' At the sound of his name, she turned back and started storming towards him. 'Heck, I'll probably still be paying off my student loans in ten years. I don't know the good restaurants to make reservations at like he would have.'

'Andy was a bastard,' she said, poking her finger into his chest. 'And he never made the reservations. I did.'

'I bet you never begged him for sex, either,' he retorted.

He felt the sting of her hand slapping his face—he probably deserved that—and refocussed his eyes on hers. Her eyes were raging, filled with fury. Her jaw was clenched, and her brow was furrowed. He shouldn't have pushed her that far, but he couldn't stop himself. He lost control of everything around her. She poked his chest again.

'You didn't have to act on it, if you didn't want to,' she said through clenched teeth, her voice shaking.

'Oh, come on, Caitlyn,' he said. 'Any man would have slept with you if you practically threw yourself at them. I'm only human.'

She stepped back, her eyes glistening. 'Is that all it was, Axel?'

'I didn't—' he started.

She let out a laugh, shaking her head and staring at the ground. 'God, I am such a fool,' she said. She looked up at him. 'And you are a jerk. I can't believe I let you make me feel like there was anything more than lust between us.'

He clenched his jaw. 'Call it what you want,' he said. 'But I felt it, too.'

'It was nothing but a superficial—' she paused, as if trying to think of the right word. 'Fling. It was a fling! There was nothing there.'

'Keep telling yourself that,' he said, his anger verging on getting the better of him.

A fling isn't exactly what he would call it. He'd had a fling before, and it was never as passionate as they'd had. A fling never involved making sure the other person was pleasantly satisfied first. And it was never with a housemate. But he'd had enough of trying to work things out with Caitlyn. Sure, he found her irresistible, and she made him feel things that he hadn't felt before, but she was infuriating. Though, he had seen the passionate side of her, and what he felt for her in those times could never be described simply as lust.

'Oh, I will,' she said.

'Fine,' he said.

'Fine!' she spat, spinning on her heel.

He watched as she walked away from him, wondering when she would remember that she'd got a lift with him. He wished it wasn't so, but it really had to be the worst date he'd been on. She had only managed to get a couple of metres away from him when someone rode past on a bicycle, wobbling dangerously close to her.

'Caitlyn, watch out!' he yelled.

But he was too late. In her effort to jump out of the way, she lost balance in her heels, falling forward. He raced towards her, feeling his heart pounding in his chest. God, if anything happened to her …

Chapter 21

She landed on her hands and knees—thank God she didn't skid—but she could feel the burning of her knees and the searing pain shooting up and down her legs. She clenched her teeth, fighting back the tears. She'd be damned if Axel saw her cry when she was trying to storm off. Trust her luck to have this happen to her. She was mad at Axel, and she didn't entirely know why. Sure, she knew that he'd said they would follow their noses. But for some reason, she'd expected that he would have at least had a plan other than walking up and down the street for so long.

She was tired. She was hungry. Her feet hurt from walking in these heels. And now, her hands and knees hurt, too. God, could this date get any worse?

She didn't even want to imagine how it could, just in case it happened. She couldn't believe that she'd slapped Axel. She hadn't meant to—not really. But she couldn't take it back once it was done. He'd looked at her so coldly after she slapped him. She didn't blame him, of course. Getting slapped isn't exactly the most romantic thing to do, and it's not really the kind of thing you want to have on a date. A first date, at that. But then, neither is bringing up exes. And she certainly didn't like that he was comparing himself with Andy.

God, Andy was a criminal. A cold-hearted, unfeeling criminal. And, of course, she never begged him for sex. She'd never found any romantic interactions particularly enjoyable with him, certainly not the way she did with Axel, anyway. Axel had a way of making her feel content. No—more than content.

Satisfied?

Complete?

She didn't think there was really a word to do justice to how he made her feel that night. She'd never found a man so irresistible, or felt as though she needed him, before. He made her feel as though she couldn't live without feeling his touch. And it didn't make sense to her. Nothing about them made sense to her.

They had never been short of conversation before the court case. They had never been at a loss for what to say. But come to think of it, most of their conversations did have something to do with the court case. She figured they might have a lull in conversation tonight because of that, but she hadn't expected that they would have fought even worse they did when they first met.

She could feel the tears building up, despite her efforts of trying to keep them at bay. She'd heard Axel tell her to watch out, but these damn heels made it impossible to do anything quickly. And now, she was kneeling on the pavement, scared to move for fear of her wounds looking worse than they felt. And possibly because she also felt as though she could die of embarrassment. She heard him yell at the biker to watch where he was going, with a few other choice words thrown in, and felt his warm touch on her elbow.

'Caitlyn, are you okay?' he asked, his voice frantic.

'I think so,' she said, cringing as she put all of her weight on her knees and looked at the palms of her hands, relieved that they weren't scratched up, just tender to the touch.

'Here, let me look,' he said, helping her to her feet.

'I'll be fi–oh!' She couldn't stop the shriek that escaped when Axel swooped his arm under her legs and started carrying her up the street. 'Axel, put me down!'

And he did, on an empty chair next to a table out in front of one of the shops. She adjusted her dress a little, trying to make it look as modest as she could manage and blushed when Axel kneeled in front of her, putting his hands on her knees. She watched as he worked, unable to find any words to say. He dusted off one of her knees before planting a gentle kiss on it.

'This one looks fine,' he said, smiling up at her.

He moved his focus over to her other knee, reached into his pocket to pull out a tissue, and started dabbing at the sore spot on her knee. She winced at the touch. He looked up at her, concern on his face.

'Does it hurt?' he asked.

'A little,' she said. 'Is it bad?'

He shook his head. 'Just a graze,' he said, continuing to dab at it with the tissue. 'It should heal nicely.' He pressed his lips to the wound and kissed it softly before looking back up at her again. 'Are you okay, Caitlyn?'

She nodded. 'I think I was just in a little bit of shock, but I'm okay,' she said.

He pulled himself up onto the other seat that was at the table, his eyes still on her. She still couldn't believe how gentle and caring he was with her knees. And she was still surprised at the strength he'd had in lifting her up so effortlessly. And she'd slapped him only moments before. It really made her look like a bitch, didn't it?

'I'm sorry I slapped you,' she said.

He shrugged, a smile on his face. 'I deserved it,' he said. 'I'm sorry I was a jerk.'

'I think you're the first person I've ever slapped,' she said.

'I think you're the only person I'm a jerk to,' he teased. She couldn't hold back the laugh, reaching over the table and giving him a little shove on his shoulder. 'We really do bring out the best in each other, don't we?'

'And the worst,' she said.

He gave her a smile that made her heart flip. God, how could they go from one end of the spectrum to the other so quickly? He held her gaze for a moment, glanced into the shop they were sitting in front of, then looked back at her, a mischievous smile on his face.

'Do you feel like pizza?' he asked.

She laughed. 'Absolutely.'

'My vote is that we take it up to the lookout.'

'The lookout?'

His eyes grew wide. 'Why do you say that as though you've never been to the lookout?'

'Because I—' she started. She what? She'd never had a reason to? She'd never had a man interested in being a romantic enough to take her there? She'd never been bothered enough to go there herself? '— I haven't.'

'Then, you don't have a choice. We're going. And we will be eating pizza while we're there,' he said.

She smiled. 'Sounds like a date,' she teased.

'Oh, it is.'

***

'I can't believe you've never been up here,' he said, sitting down on the bench next to Caitlyn and taking a slice of pizza from the box.

'I guess I never had a reason to,' she said. 'My family was never really into this kind of thing.'

He swallowed the pizza that he had in his mouth. He couldn't even imagine a life that was different to this kind of thing.

'What were they into?' he asked, taking another bite.

'Mostly just socials. Parties, dinners and the sort,' she said. 'Nothing overly adventurous or interesting.'

'That sounds terrible,' he said. 'I mean, I wouldn't enjoy that kind of lifestyle, but if that's what you like to do—'

'Oh, I hated it,' she said. 'Having to act a certain way, always working around structure. My parents had hopes that I'd be doing all of that, but I had to disappoint them by getting a degree.' She rolled her eyes.

'My family always did this kind of thing,' he said, finishing off his slice of pizza. 'While my parents were still alive, at least. We stopped doing it after Mum—' he broke off, feeling the memories resurfacing.

'Oh, Axel,' Caitlyn said, resting her hand on his thigh. 'Can I ask what happened?'

He looked into her eyes. It had been a long time since he'd told anyone exactly what had happened with his parents. And he had never properly explained it to a woman before because he hadn't had a real relationship since his parents passed away.

He had never felt close enough to any woman to share the story, and he was very selective with who he told those kinds of things to. He looked down at her hand resting gently on his thigh and placed his hand over hers, weaving his fingers between hers.

'It was a while ago,' he started. 'I was about sixteen when Mum was diagnosed with cancer. She kept getting treatment for it, and she improved for a while, but then it came back.' Her eyes widened and started to glisten. 'She fought it for three years all up before she was too weak to fight it anymore. Dad passed away within a year. He died of a broken heart.'

'I'm so sorry, Axel,' she whispered, a tear rolling down her cheek. 'God, I didn't know.'

He shrugged. 'I don't tell anyone about it,' he said. 'It's just been Tash and I since.'

She squeezed his hand. 'I'm an only child,' she said. 'Like I said, my parents were all into the social scene. We never did anything like this.' She started picking at a loose thread on the hem of her dress. 'I don't get along with my parents—I've never been able to. But I was close with my grandfather. He lived with us until he passed away, so I got to spend a lot of time with him. I used to love hearing all his stories about my grandmother. He used to say that I reminded him a lot of her. He said I had her temper and everything.'

He smiled, remembering how she easily lost her temper with him. 'I can attest to your temper,' he teased.

'Oh, shush, you,' she said, blushing, and nudging his arm.

He felt her shiver next to him and slipped his arm around her, pulling her against him. It felt as though the wind had picked up, and neither of them had jackets.

'I never got to meet her,' she said, leaning her head against his shoulder. He rested his cheek against the top of her head. 'I wish I did,' she continued. 'But I kind of feel like I already know her through his stories.'

'Imagination is a wonderful thing,' he said. She looked up at him, her eyes round and wide. 'I never met any of my grandparents, but I've heard lots of stories about them and I'm pretty sure I've made up a lot of things about them that I thought were true.'

He felt a few fat raindrops land on his arm and heard a roll of thunder. Caitlyn pulled away from him, looking up at the clouds.

'Talk about a dampener,' she said, smiling. 'I don't want to go home yet, though.'

'Do you want to sit in the car for a while?' he asked.

She nodded, rising to her feet. He picked up the pizza box and they both ran to the car, making it into the car only moments before the rain started pouring down. Of course, it wasn't exactly a dampener as Caitlyn had called it, because he'd been able to hear her adorable laugh again. He looked at her as she sat in her seat, leaning against the door, smiling at him.

'Well, I have to admit,' she started, her voice with a ring to it. 'This date has worked out to be good after all.'

He smiled. 'And you thought I was a terrible date planner.'

She laughed again, before the smile dropped from her face and she looked down at her hands that were folded in her lap. 'Can I ask you a question, Axel?' she asked.

'Shoot,' he said.

She bit her lip. 'What happened between you and Tony?'

He felt his heart race and his body stiffen, but this time, it wasn't because he didn't want to tell her what happened between them. Because, this time, he did. But he was also scared of what she would think of him when she found out the truth.

'You have to promise not to think little of me,' he said, flatly.

'Would I do that?'

He raised an eyebrow.

'Okay, I promise,' she added.

'I had two close friends when I left school—Tony and Dante,' he started. 'The three of us decided to take a gap year to figure out what we wanted to do, but we just spent most of it partying and messing around.'

'You? Partying?' Caitlyn teased. He furrowed his brow. 'Sorry,' she said quickly. 'Please, continue.'

He took a deep breath, still trying to convince himself that he did want to tell Caitlyn what happened. After all, she did deserve to know after he'd lashed out at her.

'Well, one night, we'd had a few drinks,' he said. 'Turns out that Dante had managed to sneak a few more without us knowing. We were drunk, we were stupid, it was a cold rainy night, and we were hungry.' Her eyes widened. 'At the time, I was the only one that had a car. Feeling the soberest, I figured I would drive.'

'Oh, Axel,' Caitlyn said, leaning forward a little.

He held his hand up between them. If he was going to tell her what happened, he had to say it without being interrupted, otherwise he wouldn't get it out at all. She leaned back against the door.

'Dante took my keys and jumped behind the wheel and told us that he'd leave without us if we didn't get in,' he continued. 'So, we did. And we only made it to the end of the road where he tried to speed around the corner. He lost control and I woke up in the hospital two weeks later.'

'Were you okay?' she asked, the colour drained from her face.

'Apart from being in a coma for two weeks?' he asked, shrugging. 'I got out all right. So did Tony. But Dante, he—' he broke off, staring at the rain spattering the windscreen. 'He became a paraplegic out of it. I visited him a few times, but I couldn't be around him or Tony anymore. So, I straightened myself out and studied to become a lawyer. I'm sure he blamed me for it—just got that vibe, you know?'

'You weren't the one driving, Axel,' she said. 'It's not your fault.'

He shook his head. 'It was my car, Caitlyn,' he said. 'I was supposed to be driving. That could have easily been me in the wheelchair.'

'But you're not,' she said, reaching her hand over to take hold of his. 'Axel, you can't blame yourself. None of you should have been driving, but accidents do happen. You can't beat yourself up about it.'

He lifted her hand and pressed his lips against it. He hadn't expected her to be so understanding, but he also didn't want her to pity him. She'd asked him about it, and he told her the truth.

'God, Axel, you've been through so much,' she said, her brow furrowed. 'Is that why you have had to deal with stress?'

He smiled at her abruptness, convinced that pity wasn't at the forefront of her mind. He shrugged. 'I guess so,' he said. 'I mean, that happened a short time after losing my parents.'

'I know I would struggle,' she said quietly. She looked up at him, a shimmer in her eyes. 'Axel, I know you probably think some of my methods are strange—'

'You can't convince me to do that down-doggie pose or whatever you call it,' he teased.

She smiled. 'It's called downward dog, and you might find that yoga is good for de-stressing,' she said, her voice having that cheerful ring to it that he enjoyed. 'Have you tried talking to Dante? As in, recently?'

'Not since those few times after the accident,' he admitted. 'Why?'

'Well, maybe it would help,' she said timidly. 'With healing.'

'It's been eight years and he's still in a wheelchair,' Axel said. 'I don't think visiting him would change that.'

'I didn't mean for him,' she said. He raised an eyebrow. 'You, Axel. Obviously, the whole thing has contributed to your stress. Maybe visiting him and coming to terms with the fact that it wasn't your fault would bring *you* healing.'

She touched her hand to her chest as she talked, and he sat silently until what she said caught up with him. He clenched his jaw, and shook his head.

'It's not happening,' he said, grabbing his seatbelt and locking it into place. 'If anything, it would make things worse.' A heck of a lot worse, no doubt.

'But—'

'Drop it, Caitlyn,' he said. 'It's in the past. You don't need to try to fix things. What's done is done.'

'Axel, I—'

'Caitlyn,' he warned.

'All right, I'm sorry,' she said, dropping her head as she clicked her own seatbelt into place. 'I'll stay out of it.'

Chapter 22

'Are you sure that you want to do this?' Tash passed the note to Caitlyn.

'No,' she said. 'But I know it will help him.'

Well, she hoped it would help him. She had told him that she would stay out of it, but she couldn't just sit by and watch it eat him up inside. Axel needed to find healing, and this was the only way that she could think of that he would be able to find it. She knew that Tash was hesitant to help her, but she had no one else to ask for help.

'Well, it's your relationship you're betting on. So, who am I to tell you not to?' Tash said. 'Just don't tell him that I got this for you.'

Not that they had much of a relationship to bet on. Caitlyn couldn't seem to wrap her head around what kind of a relationship they even had. Sure, they'd slept together, they fought over everything, and they seemed to have some genuinely intimate moments. But what did that make them? She figured it was just a parameter that hadn't been defined yet, but if they weren't *really* in a relationship, what did she have to lose? Okay, she could lose Axel over it. But she was betting on the opposite—even if there was only a slim chance that things could go her way.

'Thanks Tash,' she said, clutching to the note. 'I won't tell him you helped.'

***

'You're joking, right?' Axel stared at the extra pile of papers that Cameron just put on his desk.

'No one told you about the paperwork before you decided to be a lawyer, did they?' Cameron teased.

Being truthful with himself, if he'd known there was so much paperwork involved with the job, he probably would have run in the opposite direction. 'This paperwork will probably be the death of me,' he said.

'Maybe when you've been working here for as long as I have, you could hire a grad student of your own to do your paperwork.' Cameron sat opposite him. 'Until then, this is pretty much your life.'

'This isn't *all* of your paperwork, is it?'

Cameron smirked. 'What kind of a boss would I be if I gave you all of it?' he asked, leaning back in the chair, twirling a pen between his fingers. 'It's at least two-thirds of it, though. I figured you'd need a distraction after your date last night.'

Axel looked at Cameron, his brow furrowed. 'How do you know about that?'

He screwed his face up. 'Because I'm human,' he said, shrugging. 'And I saw the two of you walking down the street last night looking a bit too dressed up to just be going for a walk. Have to admit, it didn't look like it was going too well.'

Axel rolled his eyes. 'It got better,' he said. 'Then it got worse.'

'Sorry to hear it,' Cameron said. 'It sucks when you love someone, and the date doesn't go well.'

Axel blinked, Cameron's words catching up with him. Who said that love had anything to do with it? Sure, he hadn't been able to get Caitlyn out of his head since he first met her, and he'd wanted more of her the second her sweet smell of apple and cinnamon hit his nose. Once her lips touched his, he couldn't resist her—he couldn't even dream of resisting her. Especially not after he'd had her. She had a way of weaving herself into his every thought, making him feel as though she'd been around him for a lot longer than she actually had. And the chemistry between them was completely undeniable. She was irresistible, and he was so attracted to her that he lost control like he never had before.

But, love? Love was something completely different—it had to be. What they had couldn't even be close. They fought over everything, and she had a terrible habit of sticking her nose into matters that don't concern her. There was a moment in their date last night, up at the lookout, when he'd wanted to kiss her. Sure, the date had started off roughly, but there was a brief moment that he'd felt was perfect and he'd wanted to pull her close to him and kiss her. Softly, passionately—any way that he could imagine—he'd wanted to kiss her. And he should have. If he had, she might not have suggested that he should try to contact Dante. And maybe they might have ended the night on something that wasn't a total mood kill, to say the least.

'I wouldn't call it love,' Axel said, staring at his desk.

'No?' Cameron raised an eyebrow. 'I've got eyes, Axel. I've seen the way you look at Caitlyn and how you protected her when Andy assaulted her.'

'I would have done that for any woman.'

'I'm sure you would have.' Cameron shrugged. 'But not how you did for Caitlyn. Axel, it looked like you were on the verge of killing Andy and I was worried I'd have to help you hide the body. So, you might not call whatever is between you and Caitlyn love, but it's certainly not just a little crush.'

'I don't know,' Axel said, leaning back in his chair. 'Whatever it is doesn't have a chance in hell of working out, especially if she keeps meddling with things she shouldn't.'

Cameron put his pen on the desk and leaned forward. 'How so?'

'You know Jessie Turner's boyfriend, Tony?' he asked. Cameron nodded. 'I used to be friends with him years ago. He showed up at my place the night before Jessie gave her statement, bringing up a past that I'd tried to forget. And Caitlyn, well, she wants me to deal with it, thinking it'll bring healing or something of the sort.'

'Would it?'

Axel shook his head. 'I don't know. Maybe,' he said, looking up at Cameron. 'But probably not.'

'I get it,' Cameron said. 'Whatever happened in your past that you chose to ignore, it's yours to deal with. You don't have to listen to anything that anyone has to say about it.'

'Exactly.' Finally, someone who understood where he was coming from.

'But,' Cameron continued. 'If it's an issue for you and she's bringing it up to help you deal with it, cut her some slack.'

'What?' What happened to being on his side?

'She obviously cares about you.' Cameron shrugged. 'Otherwise she wouldn't give a crap about your past. If she's, as you say, meddling in your past, she's obviously serious about you.'

'She can't be serious,' Axel scoffed. 'We've only known each other a week.'

Cameron smiled, raising his eyebrows. 'You'd be surprised. It's not a matter of compatibility, Axel. It's a matter of how committed you are to making it work.'

Axel watched him pick up his pen and head towards the door before a thought occurred to him. 'Hey, Cameron?' he said. Cameron turned to face him. 'What were you doing besides watching us walk the streets?'

'I have a life, you know,' he teased. 'I was out with my fiancée.'

'You don't have a fiancée,' Axel said sceptically.

'I do now,' he said, winking.

'Really? Who?' As far as he knew, Cameron hadn't been in a serious relationship the whole time he knew him.

'The girl I knew I'd marry from the second I laid eyes on her.'

'And how long ago was that?'

Cameron tilted his head from side to side, his lips pursed in thought. 'Oh, you know,' he said. 'Three, maybe four, weeks ago.'

Axel smiled. Who was the sly dog now? 'Well, congratulations,' he said. 'I'm happy for you.'

'Thanks, man.'

'I do have one question though.' Cameron raised an eyebrow. 'How did you know, for sure?'

Cameron rolled his eyes, a broad grin plastered on his face, and started walking through the door, calling back at him. 'She meddled with my past.'

***

Caitlyn picked up her phone and put it down again. Axel would be home any minute, and with every passing moment, she was feeling increasingly like she'd stepped over a boundary. What made her think that she could pull this off? Axel told her to stay out of it. Getting Tash to find out Dante's number for her and ringing him to organise a time for Axel to come and see him was definitely not staying out of it.

Maybe she could ring him again and cancel. But that could make things even worse—especially if Axel did, one day, want to make amends with him. God, she'd really screwed up. Why did she have to stick her nose where it didn't belong? She never thought she was the kind of person to do it, but since both Andy and Axel had said it to her in the last week, maybe she was. Come to think of it, her grandfather had always said that she tended to involve herself with other people's business. But she'd thought that she'd grown out of it—thought it was just something that would only last for the length of her childhood. She guessed some things don't change.

Saying that, she was certain that Andy was overreacting, and now, she could see that he had something to hide. So, of course, he would want her to stay out of his business. But Axel? She didn't know why she was so concerned about this. Like he'd said, it was in the past, and it definitely wasn't her place to try to fix it. She'd made a mistake, calling Dante. A mistake fuelled by boredom of being cooped up in this house with no one but Flop, of not being able to work until her leave ended, of not really having anything to do except being left with her thoughts.

She could feel her heart racing. God, she had to undo what she'd done. She'd been selfish thinking that Axel might appreciate this kind of gesture. She should never have thought that he wouldn't, by any means, know how he really felt about it. She should never have assumed that he might take her meddling lightly. Oh God, she was a meddler! How had she become a meddler? It was one thing to stick her nose where it didn't belong, but another to actually get involved with it.

She picked up the phone and started punching in Dante's number. She had to cancel. If she managed to cancel before Axel got home, she might not have to tell him about it—ever—and they could move on. She could keep out of it, let him make his own decisions regarding it and maybe—*maybe*—they could go on another date that ends a bit better than last night. Preferably, a lot better than last night.

She got about half-way through punching in the numbers when she heard the key click in the front door and watched Flop jump up from his spot and bolt towards the door. She cancelled the numbers and stuffed the note with his details into her pocket, leaping towards the couch to look as though she wasn't doing anything suspicious.

'Hey, sleepyhead,' he said, closing the door behind him.

Oh, that's right—she'd pretended to be asleep again when he went to work. How could she face him when she already knew what she would be doing today?

'Hey, how was work?' she asked.

'Cumbersome. Glad it's the weekend, though.' He squinted at her. 'What's wrong?'

'Nothing,' she said quickly. Maybe she could cancel with Dante while Axel was in the shower or something. He would never have to know.

'Do I have something on my face?'

'No.'

'Then, why do you look suspicious?'

'I don't look suspicious,' she defended.

He opened his mouth as if to say something more, then closed it, and moved towards the bench where Caitlyn had put the mail for him. 'Damn bills,' he said, pushing the letters to the side. Then, he picked up a small piece of paper and read over it, turning to face Caitlyn. 'What the hell is this?'

Her eyes widened, and she pulled the scrunched-up paper from her pocket, feeling her heart drop to her stomach when she realised that she'd shoved a receipt into her pocket, not Dante's details.

'Why do you have Dante's details?' he continued.

'I thought you might change your mind,' she said, hesitantly.

'Well, I haven't,' he said, his brow furrowed. 'And why did you involve Tash with this?'

'I didn't,' she lied.

He held up the paper in front of him. 'I know my sister's handwriting, Caitlyn.'

'I promised I wouldn't tell,' she said, defeatedly.

'And you promised me you would stay out of it,' he retorted, unbuttoning his shirt as he moved towards his room.

'I'm sorry.' She stood, following him.

He shook his head. 'I don't think you are,' he said. 'You didn't call him, did you?'

She grimaced. She'd thought that he might have at least considered it at first. And even though she'd convinced herself it was a bad idea right before he got home, she still had a little bit of hope that he might still consider it. Apparently not.

'Caitlyn!'

He turned, surprising her as she almost walked into him. He was mere inches away from her, and his exposed chest made her want to reach out and touch him. Maybe seducing him would soften the blow? Without thinking, she reached her hand out to touch his chest, but he stopped her hand before she could, gripping her wrist.

'What did you say to him?' he growled through gritted teeth.

She could feel her heart breaking, but she couldn't understand why. Did she really feel for him so much that he already had the power to hurt her? 'I said that you wanted to see him,' she whispered.

His eyes rounded. 'Why the *hell* would you say that?'

'I thought you might have just needed a nudge,' she said.

He let go of her wrist, taking a step backwards, spreading his arms out. 'It didn't occur to you that I legitimately didn't want to see him again?' Flop whimpered at their feet. Great, even his dog agreed with him. 'You didn't organise a time, did you?' he continued.

She plastered a smile on her face to try to soften the blow, knowing that she probably looked more like she was in pain. 'Tomorrow,' she said hesitantly. 'At three-thirty.'

'God, Caitlyn!' He closed the door between them and she rested her head against the doorframe. 'Stay out of it, Caitlyn. It's a simple instruction, don't you think?' he continued.

'I'm sorry, Axel,' she said through the door. 'I didn't think—'

'Oh, it sounds like it's been consuming your thoughts since Tony showed up,' he retorted.

She bit her lip, fighting back the tears. Why didn't she see this coming before it was too late? It's like she couldn't get anywhere with Axel, even if she desperately wanted to. He opened the door, dressed in his workout gear.

'Nothing to say to that?' he asked, his eyes cold.

'I'm sorry,' she whispered, hoping that the coolness in his eyes could disappear if he saw how sincere she was. 'I was just trying to help.'

His eyes narrowed, glaring at her intensely, his eyes boring into her. He made her nervous.

'Well, don't,' he growled.

She watched him leave, Flop following at his heels. God, she really screwed up.

She'd crossed a line.

Bringing it up and trying to get him to talk about it was one thing, but arranging something with Dante behind his back was another. She had no right to dig into his past like that and make decisions. It didn't affect her. If she'd left it alone, it wouldn't affect her. Now, she'd thrown herself into the things he'd tried to leave in his past and he had no choice but to deal with it.

Axel felt the jar through his body as his feet pounded on the ground, Flop running at his heels. He could feel his heart beating rhythmically against his chest, his breath quickening, his muscles firing. And the faster he ran, the more he pushed himself to go harder. But he still couldn't get Caitlyn out of his head. God, how was he supposed to straighten out his thoughts—and his life—with her meddling with his past?

In just a little over a week, she'd occupied his thoughts so much that he couldn't even imagine how he lived before meeting her. How was that possible? If she was to disappear out of his life now, he could never forget her. He would still think about her all the time. And he would probably struggle to adjust to life without her. But he shouldn't feel like that. If anything, it was a whirlwind romance. It had the power to go incredibly well, or terribly wrong. And he didn't have the faintest idea as to where it would end up, but he knew where he wanted it to go. He kept pushing until he couldn't push any more, and stopped to catch his breath, leaning against a tree, Flop running a circle around him before sitting at the base of the tree.

He thought about what Cameron had said to him—could he be right? He'd never thought that it was possible to develop feelings so strong for someone so quickly. But now, with Caitlyn? Love was a strong word, and he couldn't be sure that that was what he felt for her. How could he be sure? All he knew was that he'd never felt like that for anyone else before. Caitlyn was special, unique. And she stirred something inside of him that he just couldn't ignore.

He looked around him to take in the scene, his eyes focussing on the bench where he'd bumped into Caitlyn on her wedding day. He smiled at the memory of Flop leading him to her that day, their exchange at the chemist, and of course, their encounter at the café. Could it really be a coincidence that he'd bumped into her at three entirely unrelated places in such a short time frame? And could it be chance that he'd been working on a case that involved her for weeks before he even met her? He'd been working towards putting her fiancé away for good, and the thought that the bastard may have been involved with someone so endearing and special as Caitlyn—or anyone at all, for that matter—hadn't even occurred to him. How could he explain why Flop had run off that day and managed to find the jilted bride on this bench?

He couldn't. He couldn't explain any of it—their fights, their passion, their chance encounters. Her meddling with his past, and him meddling with hers. He laughed at the irony. All this time, he had been working towards putting the man she was involved with behind bars. He'd been bringing up her past, and the hurts that she'd tried to hide. He'd made her face the man she'd spent all of her adult life with and testify against him. And now he was frustrated about her bringing up his past. He might not be sure whether him meeting Caitlyn was a coincidence, or if there was a greater force involved, but he was convinced that finding a bride on this park bench was the exact moment that his life really changed, and everything he knew was turned upside down.

But seeing Dante after so long? Was he ready to open that box again? Could it really help him move on with his life, or would it set him back again? Flop whimpered, pawing at his feet. He reached down and scratched Flop's ear.

'I get it, Flop,' he said. 'I know what I have to do.'

***

Caitlyn followed her hand with her eyes as she ran her fingertips over the beaded front of her wedding dress, still hanging in the wardrobe. God, how she'd thought it was perfect. Every little detail was perfect. Or at least, it was supposed to be. But her fiancé had to be involved with multiple murders, get her best friend pregnant, and turn out to be a complete and total ass. The once-white tone was still speckled with muddy patches from Flop's paws and that dress that was supposed to make her feel like a princess was nothing more than its name implied—a dress. A big, poufy, overpriced, overrated dress that meant nothing to her. Or, so she thought.

She swallowed the threatening tears. This damn dress still represented the life she could have had. She could have been married, secure in a relationship, knowing exactly what was going to happen with her relationship tomorrow. But while she envisioned that life that she was so close to having, Andy wasn't the man she pictured herself with. If anything, he made her sick to her stomach, and she doubted that feeling would ever ease.

She had never even been close to being in that kind of a relationship with Axel, yet he was the one she pictured herself with. She knew that it was too early to even entertain the idea. After all, she wouldn't exactly call what they have a secure relationship. And she definitely didn't know what would be happening with it tomorrow, or even if she would still be living with Axel, or if she'd be out on her own trying to find somewhere to go. Surely, Axel wouldn't cast her out on her own? Otherwise he would never have invited her to stay with him and Tash to start with. But she didn't feel as though she would be comfortable staying if she'd screwed up everything that they might have had between them, especially after being so … intimate … with each other.

She scratched at a bit of dried mud on the hem of the dress. Maybe, one day, she would have a second chance at love, and maybe it would work out for her instead of going terribly wrong. And as much as she pictured being with Axel and wishing desperately that he was the one that she'd had that chance with, she couldn't force anything if they weren't made for each other. Even if it would break her heart to say goodbye. She could already feel her heart aching at the thought of it, and the knowledge that she'd truly screwed up didn't help. This time, Axel had every reason to hate her for going behind his back. And she couldn't blame him if he did.

Caitlyn heard a soft knock on her bedroom door, brushed away the stray tears and closed the wardrobe door. She heard her door jar open and turned to face it.

'Caitlyn?' Axel whispered. 'Can I come in?'

She swiped at her face again, making sure that there was no dampness left on her cheeks, hesitating. 'Sure.'

He swung the door open and moved slowly towards her, Flop resting just outside her door. 'I hope I wasn't interrupting anything.' He indicated towards the wardrobe.

She followed his eyes, finding the wardrobe door slightly ajar with part of the poufy wedding dress poking out. She blushed, pushing it back into the wardrobe in a second attempt to hide it. 'Oh, I was just ... thinking,' she mumbled.

He turned her to face him, nudging her chin up and locking eyes with hers. 'You've been crying,' he whispered. 'Are you okay?'

She swallowed, her mouth dropping open before she snapped it shut. She couldn't tell Axel that she'd been envisioning herself in a white dress—obviously not the same one in her wardrobe, of course—walking down the aisle towards him. Or, should she say, she was dreaming, because it would likely never happen.

His eyes were saddened, his brows scrunching closer together. 'I'm sorry I snapped at you.'

'You had every right to.' She dropped her gaze, looking down at the hand that was wrapped around hers. 'I was out of line.'

'You were,' he said, surprising her. She looked up, catching his eyes again, her forehead crinkled. Before she could retort, he pressed his thumb to her lips. 'But you were right.'

'What?'

He shrugged. 'I shouldn't have been so quick to reject your idea. You made a fair point—odds are, Dante probably does blame himself more than he blames me. But whether or not he blames me for how he is now, he deserves an apology.'

Her mouth dropped open and he nudged her chin with his index finger to close it. 'What changed your mind?' she whispered.

A smile tugged at his lips. 'You were never going to stay out of it, were you?'

She shook her head, dropping her gaze. 'I guess it's a bad habit of mine.'

He moved his head so that he could catch her eyes again. 'I don't think it's so bad,' he whispered. She could feel the warmth radiating from his body. 'So, I'm doing it for you.'

Her eyes widened as she looked up at him again. 'You mean—'

'I'll go see Dante tomorrow.' He brushed the tips of his fingers across her cheek, tucking her hair behind her ear. 'Under one condition.'

She jerked back, searching his face. Who said anything about conditions? That was something that she hadn't expected—the whole conversation was unexpected. She'd crossed a line, she knew it, and she'd expected that it would have been the end of them. She didn't anticipate that he would agree to do it. The thought that he might have thrown in a condition never even crossed her mind, and it made her nervous.

'And what would that be, Mr Taylor?'

She swallowed, waiting for his answer for what seemed like an eternity. He straightened his body, his eyes stern, but somehow playful, and held her just below her shoulders.

'You have to forgive Sophia,' he said. 'And make amends with her.'

***

He tried to keep a straight face, but inside, he was smirking. He didn't particularly want to see Dante tomorrow—or ever, for that matter. But he also couldn't stand the thought of not having Caitlyn in his life. So, he'd thought of the one thing that she would be least likely to want to do. Sophia, once her best friend, was pregnant with Caitlyn's ex-fiancé's baby and she found out on her wedding day. Who would forgive that? Maybe with time, she could get past it. But overnight? She was on a limited time frame if she wanted him to see Dante tomorrow. At the very least, he'd bought himself some time.

He nudged her mouth closed again, not for the first time in this conversation, and took in the shocked look that was plastered on her face.

'You're joking, right?' she said, hesitantly.

He shrugged. 'That's the condition.'

She backed up, shaking her head. 'You can't ask me to do that.'

'Why not?' He followed her, matching every one of her steps backwards with a step forward of his own. 'You're asking me to talk to Dante.'

'That's different.'

'How?'

Her eyes were wide, rounded, her eyebrows arched high. 'Because Dante's not pregnant with your ex-fiancé's child.'

'No, but he is a paraplegic and it happened on my watch.' He took her by the shoulders. 'Caitlyn, being pregnant and being a paraplegic are both life-changing and they both affect everyone in your life. So, although they might not be exactly the same, and can by no means compare with each other, they both still affect each of us the same.'

'But—' Her mouth opened and closed a few times. 'You've had more time to get used to it.'

He spread his arms out, a smirk on his face. 'Take it or leave it, princess. But that's the condition.' He gave her arm a pat. 'You forgive Sophia and make amends with her, and I'll make amends with Dante.'

She tightened her lips and swallowed. She wasn't happy about his condition—he could tell. But she was also considering it, and that made him feel that he'd made a real gamble with it. Of course, if she accepted and went through with her part of the condition, he would follow through with his—he would owe that to her even if he wasn't entirely enthused about the idea. After all, he was asking a lot of her. She was right—he'd had years to come to terms with the idea of Dante as a paraplegic. She'd only had a week.

She shifted her weight to one foot, her arms crossed, her brows crinkled, her lips still tight. God, she looked adorable. He wanted to ask her to forget any part of the arrangement and take her now—to taste the sweetness of her lips and feel her body move with his. But he had to refrain. They'd taken it too far too quickly already and he couldn't let that happen again. Not when she could still leave at a moment's notice.

'Fine.'

'You mean—'

'I'll do it. But,' she said, raising her finger between them, tapping him on the nose, 'you are a jackass.'

Chapter 24

'Having second thoughts already?'

Caitlyn jumped, spinning to face Axel who was standing dangerously close to her. 'What the hell are you doing?'

He reached his hand out towards the door she was standing in front of. 'You've been standing here for the last five minutes just staring at the door. I'm reminding you that if you back out, I don't go to see Dante.'

'You'd like that, wouldn't you?' She was sure he would. He still didn't seem enthused about making amends with Dante, but he'd made a deal with her. She had to make amends with Sophia first, then he would go to the meeting she'd set up with Dante. She sure as hell wasn't going to be backing out now.

She had too much pride to do that. 'I was just working out what I would say. Go, wait in the car like you said you would.'

He nudged her shoulder with his, his eyebrows raised and a sly grin on his face, then he walked back to the car. She took a deep breath, turning back to the door and knocked. Why on earth did she care so much about him making amends with Dante that she had convinced herself that she could bring herself to do the same with Sophia? It wasn't fair, and it wasn't the same, even if Axel was convinced that it was. He'd had more time to prepare himself for it than she did. But it wasn't entirely Sophia's fault—she had to tell herself that. Andy was a jerk, a player, and a criminal. And the idea of him was hard to resist. She knew—she'd been there.

But this? She wasn't ready for this. She'd talked to Sophia the other day because it was out of necessity. Sophia was in real danger then. But now, Andy was being held in police custody and soon enough, he would be behind bars. She felt her heart pounding in her chest as she turned quickly and took the steps off the veranda as quickly as she could. Axel would think she's a coward—she felt like a coward. But why should he care? He would get out of having to see Dante.

'Caitlyn?'

The weak voice stopped her in her tracks. She closed her eyes briefly and turned back to the girl who used to be her best friend, standing in the doorway, looking as pale as snow, her eyes misted, and skinnier than usual.

'Are you coming inside?' Sophia asked.

Caitlyn nodded, hesitantly, and urged her feet to move her forward until she was standing in Sophia's house, the curtains all closed, the only light coming from a dull lamp in the corner next to a pedestal fan pointed at the couch. She turned around, surprised to see how sunken Sophia's face was starting to look.

'God, Soph, you look terrible!' She hadn't meant to blurt it out that way. Surely, she could have found a more tactful way to say it.

Sophia rolled her eyes and took up a seat on the couch. Caitlyn sat next to her, noticing a bucket on the floor once her eyes had adjusted. 'Morning sickness, for the most part,' Sophia said. 'The knowledge that it's his just seems to make it worse.' She put a damp cloth on her forehead, closing her eyes, and leaning her head back against the couch.

Caitlyn kept her mouth shut. How was she supposed to respond to that? Caitlyn had always thought that she was pretty tough. But she'd also always seen Sophia as a strong woman—probably more than she felt she was. And here she was, visibly breaking apart, her body deteriorating, going through an even bigger hell than Caitlyn had been going through.

'Why are you here, Caitlyn?'

Caitlyn's eyes shot up to catch Sophia staring at her. Even her normally deep blue eyes had faded to an almost grey. 'I came to check on you,' she whispered.

Sophia shook her head slowly. 'My own family has practically disowned me, Caitlyn,' she said, her voice shaking. 'Not because I'm pregnant, but because I got pregnant with my best friend's fiancé. I am carrying a criminal's child, and I'm suffering because of it. So, forgive me if I don't believe you. My own family doesn't give a damn about me. Why should you?'

Caitlyn shuffled to the edge of the couch, taking Sophia's hand in hers. 'I still care about you, Sophia. You've been my best friend for longer than I can remember. That doesn't just go away.'

Sophia's eyes were filled with tears. 'I hurt you, Caitlyn, bad. That kind of puts a pretty big wedge between us. I wouldn't forgive me, if I were you.'

'Which is why you're not me,' she said. 'I'm not saying that it didn't hurt. It did—does—a lot. But it worked out okay in the end. Just think'—she held the tips of her index finger and her thumb an inch apart from each other—'I was this close to being married to a criminal. You saved me, Soph.'

'I still don't see how that makes it okay.'

'It doesn't.' Caitlyn shrugged. 'But it does make it easier to forgive you. Andy has a way of convincing you to do things in the moment that you might not otherwise do. He's a jerk and the idea of being with someone so well-known would appeal to anyone. So, I don't blame you. He's the one at fault.'

Sophia swallowed, wiping the tears from her eyes. 'Do you mean that?'

Caitlyn nodded.

'I don't deserve it,' Sophia continued. 'But thank you.'

'Of course,' Caitlyn said. 'But I do have to ask— why did you do it?'

A faint smile played at her lips. 'Because I'm an idiot. I was jealous, and lonely, and he played me like a fool.'

Caitlyn leant back against the couch. 'You're not the only one,' she said. 'He had me believing that he actually loved me that whole time.'

'I am really sorry,' Sophia said.

'I know.'

'I know it's really not any of my business,' Sophia continued after a moment of silence between them. 'But you and the lawyer, huh?'

Caitlyn blushed, but she didn't move, nor did she say anything. Sophia stared at the fan. 'I'm happy for you, I really am. You deserve to be happy.' She turned to look at Caitlyn. 'And you actually suit each other. Isn't he the guy you spilled coffee on?'

Her blush deepened. 'Yes, he is.'

Sophia smiled. 'That's sweet. And totally a keeper.'

'What do you mean by that?' Caitlyn asked, her eyebrow lifted.

'A man who's willing to put another guy behind bars for you is worth keeping, don't you think?'

'He didn't do it for me,' Caitlyn defended. 'He did it for Faith. Her father is the one who was suing Andy.'

'Maybe so,' Sophia continued. 'But you're the one who gave him a real reason to pull every string he could to put Andy where he belongs. I'm happy that you found someone to be with. It gives me a bit of hope.'

'Oh, we're not together,' Caitlyn said, her eyes wide. 'Not really.'

'But you love him, right?'

Caitlyn's mouth dropped open. 'I wouldn't … ahh … call it that …'

'Oh, come on,' Sophia said, nudging Caitlyn's arm. 'It's so obvious! I saw the way you looked at him at the hearing—you're in love. And I would bet a million that he loves you, too.'

She felt her lips tightening, her stomach stirring. In love? With Axel Taylor? It couldn't possibly be true. She'd never once thought of that word to describe what they had. But maybe it was the one word she'd been looking for this whole time.

***

'So, when are you seeing her next?' Axel pulled into his driveway, waiting for an answer that didn't come. He turned in his seat to face her. 'Caitlyn?'

Her eyes shot towards him, confusion written all over her face. 'Seriously?' he said. 'What did she say to you in there? You've been out of it all the way home.'

Her brows crinkled, her expression apologetic. 'I'm sorry, Axel,' she said. 'I'm just thinking about something she said.'

'What was it?'

She shook her head. 'It doesn't matter. The point is, I held up my end of the deal, so now it's your turn. Are you sure you don't want me to come with you?'

Her evasiveness didn't go unnoticed, but he didn't have the time to bring it up. It would just have to wait until later—along with all the conversations related to them. He shook his head. 'No, I have to do this myself.' He flashed a smile. 'After all, how would it make me look if I was to bring you with me, after you just made things right with Sophia by yourself?'

She raised an eyebrow. 'I suppose a bit of a coward, wouldn't it?'

'Hey, you almost ran away from dealing with Sophia,' he teased. 'And you would have got away with it if she hadn't opened the door.'

'But I still did it,' she said, nudging his arm. 'And now it's your turn, Mr Taylor, before it's too late.'

He waited until she was inside before pulling out of the driveway and starting the hour and a half trip north of Goulburn to the address on the note that Caitlyn had scribbled on. He wondered if she would know if he didn't see Dante. She would. He couldn't know for sure how much she would figure out, but he did know that he was a terrible liar, especially to someone he loved. That was another thing. He was falling—too hard, too fast—for Caitlyn. And he couldn't do anything to hurt her. It would near on kill him if he did. Like she said, she completed her part of the deal. Now, it was his turn.

***

'Tony?'

Axel blinked. What the hell was Tony doing here? He'd said that he stopped visiting Dante years ago. So, why was he here, at Dante's house, when Axel was supposed to be visiting him?

'What are you doing here?'

'I live here,' Tony said, shrugging.

'But Dante—'

'Lives here, too,' Tony finished.

'You said that you stopped visiting him years ago,' Axel said, trying to make sense of it all.

'I *did* stop visiting,' Tony said. 'When I moved in.'

'Are you serious?'

Tony nodded. 'Since you weren't around, you probably never heard that his mum passed.'

'I had heard.'

'And you never cared to visit?' Tony asked. Axel stared at him. Was he still trying to make him feel guilty for not visiting? 'Anyway,' Tony continued. 'He still needed company and since his mum wasn't around, I took it upon myself to be that person.'

'How very charitable of you,' Axel said flatly. He had never known a charitable bone in Tony.

Tony shrugged. 'Can't say the same for you.' He moved aside to let Axel through the door. 'But, for some obscure reason, he still wanted to see you all those years.'

Axel eyed him sceptically. 'So, what else have you lied about?'

'Just that,' he said, shrugging. 'Oh, and I didn't get your details from Tash. I saw you down the street and followed you home. I waited for a while, of course, to make sure it was your place you went to which gave me enough time to come up with an excuse that didn't make me sound like a stalker.' Axel's eyes widened. Tony indicated towards the lounge and started walking in the opposite direction. 'Better not keep him waiting.'

'You're not coming in?' Axel stared at the door leading to the lounge.

'Oh, his royal highness requested a private visitation.'

Axel raised an eyebrow and waited until Tony was out of sight. 'Here goes nothing,' he said, opening the door.

Dante was sitting in his wheelchair, his back towards him, looking out the window through the crack of the curtains. The room was dark except for the bit of light coming through the window and smelled musty as though it hadn't been aired out in years. He didn't turn to face him.

'I wondered when you would bother to visit,' Dante said, his voice deep, sorrowful.

Axel squinted, trying to encourage his eyes to adjust to the poor lighting. Those few times that he did see Dante in the hospital, his room was darkened like this. He wondered if he'd continued living like this since then. Dante turned his head to the side where Axel could see his profile. The shape of his face looked hollowed, solemn, and something else that he couldn't pinpoint the nature of.

'Just like the last time I saw you then? Nothing to say?'

'What do you want me to say, Dante? That I'm sorry I never visited?'

'That would be a good start.' Dante turned his wheelchair slowly so that he was facing Axel.

'I was always a second-class citizen to you, Dante,' Axel said, taking a step forward. 'And that never changed after the accident. Why would I hang around and be treated like crap?' He could see Dante's jaw clench in his silhouette. When would his eyes adjust?

'I will never walk again because of you.'

Axel straightened, pointing his finger at him. 'You were the one driving, remember?'

'It was your car,' Dante growled. 'You weren't as drunk as I was. You should have never given me the keys.'

For eight years, Axel had blamed himself for what happened with Dante. Eight years of his life, he'd felt guilty. And he'd wasted all that time and energy blaming himself. Hearing Dante say it, he realised that he was never the one to blame.

'That's not fair. You took the keys off me.'

Dante spread his arms out. 'It's your word against mine.'

Axel shook his head, putting his hand on the door handle. 'I never should have come here. I was right to walk away from you all those years ago. You know, Caitlyn actually had me believing that you would have blamed yourself all this time.'

'She was wrong.' His voice was sinister.

'And all this time, I actually blamed myself for your condition,' he continued, staring at the ground. 'But you know what? There's no one to blame but yourself.'

Axel heard a distinctive click and shot his head up towards Dante, just in time to watch him pull the trigger. But he was too late to do anything. He struggled to breathe, and his body felt as though it was on fire. Dante was looking at him, his eyes burning with hate, a slither of smoke rolling out of the muzzle of his pistol. Axel looked down at his chest, blood staining his shirt, and felt himself falling towards the ground but didn't feel the impact of hitting it. Tony's voice was the second last thing he heard.

'Dante, no!'

The sound of the pistol shooting again was the last.

Chapter 25

Caitlyn glanced at the time again and eyed the meal that she'd made to surprise Axel. Lasagne—his favourite, according to Tash—with a garden salad garnished with shallots and feta cheese, with bread and butter pudding waiting to go into the oven. She'd found the guava-scented candles that she'd packed in her honeymoon bag and peeled the stickers off them that had her and Andy's initials on them. No point in letting the candles go to waste, right?

She'd changed into a pretty dress, set the table with the lasagne and salad in the middle, dimmed the lights, lit the candles, and waited. Axel should have been home by now. He said that he would be home by six and well, that was half an hour ago. It was only half an hour, right? He would probably be on his way home. She figured it must have gone well with Dante, otherwise Axel would have been home even earlier. He didn't strike her as one to hang around if it wasn't going well, so it was obviously a good sign that he was late home. She wasn't entirely bothered about it. Disappointed, yes, that the lasagne was getting cold and the salad was getting warm and the bread and butter pudding was getting soggy. But he didn't know that she was going to surprise him with a home date, and if he'd patched things up with Dante, they'd have a lot to catch up on.

She thought about what Sophia said. Surely, she didn't love Axel—it was too soon. Falling in love so quickly was just a fairy tale, right? Well, that's what she'd grown to believe, but Sophia had always believed in fairy tales. Sure, she liked Axel—a lot. And she was definitely attracted to him. And after their night together, she couldn't believe that she'd ever settled for Andy. But maybe it was the timing. She may have never met Axel if she wasn't planning to marry Andy. She'd called it lust, what her and Axel had. And he was everything she needed in a man— someone to set her on the right path, who valued friendship enough to encourage her to make amends with Sophia, to treat her right. Maybe, one day, they would fall in love. But since Andy won't be bothering her anymore and their previous disagreements with their friends had been settled, they had all the time in the world to explore their relationship. They could take things as fast or as slow as they wanted. There was nothing stopping them.

He was a man who challenged her in the right ways and was willing to come to a compromise when they couldn't agree on something. He had something that she'd never known in Andy. But love? Sure, her feelings were strong. But she was still set in her decision that love didn't come this easily. She'd wasted another fifteen minutes thinking, and Axel still wasn't home. But she shouldn't be worried. She didn't want to be the overly controlling girlfriend. Girlfriend—that was another title she'd jumped to. Really, they weren't at that stage yet. But she'd hoped to get there tonight. But something in her gut was telling her that she should be worried. She tried calling his mobile, but it rung out. Sighing, she turned the lights back on, blew out the candles, and put the food in the fridge—it would all go bad if it sat on the table for much longer.

She started moving towards her room to change out of her dress—she felt pathetic, dolling herself up like this—and was startled when she heard a knock on the door. She moved towards it. Maybe Axel forgot his key? There was another knock, rapid and furious.

'Caitlyn, open up!' The voice was shaking.

She swung the door open. 'Tash?'

Tash's expression was concerned, scared, her eyes puffy. 'I forgot my phone and the spare key in my rush to get out of the house.' Her voice was wavering. 'We have to go—now.'

Tash turned on her heel and started walking back towards her car—the engine still running, Liam in the driver's seat. Caitlyn grabbed her bag, dropping her phone and the spare key into it and pulled the front door closed behind her, checking that it was locked.

'Tash, wait!' she called. 'Why do we have to go?'

Tash paused, one hand on the roof of the car and the other on the open door. 'Axel's been shot. Dante shot him.'

Axel's been shot. Her feet stopped moving and she felt the blood draining from her body. How could that happen? Dante had seemed so excited on the phone to hear that Axel would be coming to visit. She thought—oh, God. He'd planned it. And she had made it possible for him. If she had just stayed out of it like Axel had asked her to …

'Caitlyn, come on!'

She wiped at the tears that fell freely down her face and forced her legs to move, sitting in the back of the car. Liam started driving before she could even click the seatbelt into place. 'Is he okay?' she forced out, not recognising her own voice.

'He's critical,' Tash said, staring at her hands in her lap. 'That's all they could tell me on the phone.'

Finally managing to click the seatbelt into place, Caitlyn leaned her head back against the car seat. God, this was all her fault. She shouldn't have been so presumptuous. Axel hadn't seen Dante in eight years. She had no place to try to fix things between them. It's because of her that Axel got shot. And now, she may lose him.

The ride to the hospital was the hardest ride of her life. None of them knew where he got shot, how bad it really was, what could happen. And the ache that penetrated right down to the depths of her stomach wasn't enough to prepare her for what the doctor said when Tash finally convinced someone to talk.

'We did everything we could. Be prepared that he might not make it.'

***

She had no idea how many hours had passed before she could see him, but when she finally did, she felt that ache deepen. Her knees buckled as she tried to sit on the seat near his bed and she tenderly took his hand in hers. It seemed like he was hooked to so many machines that beeped rhythmically and a large surgical bandage covered the corner just below his left shoulder and the top of his chest. The doctors had told them that the bullet had narrowly missed his arteries, but he'd still lost a lot of blood. His chances of surviving were better now that he was out of surgery, but there was always that risk. She couldn't focus on anything the doctor said after that.

'Axel, can you hear me?' she whispered.

She waited for him to open his eyes or squeeze her hand—anything. But it didn't happen. She stroked back his hair that was sticking to his clammy forehead and kissed his hand before resting her head on it.

'I'm so sorry,' she said, shaking her head, her tears wetting their hands. 'I shouldn't have encouraged you to go. I didn't know ...' She paused, thinking that she felt his finger twitch, but convinced herself that she was imagining it. 'Dante killed himself, Axel, after he shot you.' She choked on the words. 'Tony had no idea that he'd planned it. God, I don't know what I would do if you ...'

She couldn't finish the sentence. Partly because she couldn't bring herself to even think about him dying, but also because what Sophia said still rung in her mind. *She loved him.* If she didn't, she wouldn't have vowed to not leave his side until he woke up. She knew that sleep would be impossible and that she couldn't go home—not without him. Sophia was right. Even if Caitlyn didn't believe in falling for someone so quickly before, it was hard to deny when it was staring you in the face. She loved Axel, and there was no point in denying it anymore. She wiped at her eyes, looking up at his face, still unconscious, still unmoving.

'I love you, Axel,' she whispered. 'I hope you can hear me, but if you can't, I'll keep telling you when you wake up. God, I hope you don't think I'm a fool, but I—'

She broke off one last time, the machine that he was hooked to flatlining, and before she knew it, she was being ushered out of the room that was quickly filling with hospital staff and her heart was shattering to a million pieces.

***

Axel never thought that your life actually flashed before your eyes when you were dying. That was, until he was experiencing it. He saw everything—from his first day at school, his first broken bone, his first kiss, and Tash's first heartbreak, to the struggle that he and his family went through with his mother's illness and losing his father shortly after, his adventures with Tony and Dante and their accident, his experiences at university. Everything that he could remember seemed to flash before his eyes so quickly—like a film on fast-forward—until it stopped playing and he was left with an image that he'd never seen before.

Caitlyn.

She was in a white flowing dress, her copper-brown hair rolling in waves over her shoulders and down her back, her feet were bare. She had her back towards him and was delicately handling a blossom on an almond tree that looked untouched. He felt his body moving towards her, her sweet cinnamon and apple scent reaching him when he was still a few feet away. She turned to face him, her face glowing—in fact, everything seemed to be glowing—and they were surrounded with various shades of white and not much else. *Where were they?*

'I was wondering when you would join me,' she said, her voice sweet.

She took his hand and led him to a bench seat, and they sat, their surroundings changing. He recognised the bench as the one that he'd found her crying on the day of her wedding.

'Do you remember?' she asked tentatively.

He looked up at her, questioningly. Did he remember every encounter they had had together? Did he remember the night they spent making love? Did he remember the feeling that he felt when Andy Graeme was found guilty and he knew that Caitlyn could finally be his? Of course he did. He couldn't forget anything to do with her—her touch, her scent, he had committed everything about her to his memory. He nodded.

'Do you think there was a reason we went through everything we did? So that we could be brought together?'

He nodded again. He'd always been sceptical of it before, but after today, he was certain that they were meant for each other. She touched her hand to his chest, rolling her finger over the scar from the bullet. He grimaced.

'Does it still hurt?'

He tried to speak, but he couldn't form any words, so he nodded again. It shouldn't though, right? Not if it was a scar now. But then, this wasn't real. It couldn't be real. He heard her voice again, but her mouth wasn't moving. It was as though a narrator was speaking in an obscure, very realistic dream.

'I love you, Axel,' the voice said. It sounded desperate, shaky.

Caitlyn took her hand away from his chest like she'd been electrocuted and stood to her feet. 'You have to go now.'

He tried to speak again, but there were still no words. And as he watched her, and their surroundings, disappear to leave him standing in pure white, he felt a burning through his chest—an ache at first, but one that intensified so quickly that he could hear a scream, as if it were his own, but he couldn't tell if it was his. The white faded in a split-second and he opened his eyes, coughing and gasping for air, trying to discern his new surroundings. Scrubs. Wires. Concerned eyes.

'Glad to see you're back with us, Mr Taylor,' one of the scrubs said.

He looked around, still trying to form words that weren't coming.

The nurse checked his pulse, nodding at the scrubs that talked. 'You were shot, Axel. You've had surgery and you're on the mend. But we thought we'd lost you there for a while. You weren't responding.' He wasn't responding? He … died? 'You gave your girlfriend quite the fright.' *Caitlyn*. 'Would you like to see her now?'

He nodded. 'Yes,' he said, not recognising his raspy voice. He had to see Caitlyn.

The nurses cleaned him up and propped him up in his bed before letting Caitlyn come in. And when he laid his eyes on her, it was as though he was seeing her for the first time. She was a vision. She wore a blue knee-length dress, her face made-up, but smudged around her eyes that glistened with fresh tears, her hair rolling over her shoulders. She moved quicker than he'd ever seen her move before and she held his face between her hands kissing his lips, his eyes, his nose.

'Oh, God, Axel, you're all right. You're going to be all right,' she said, her voice shaking. He felt the sting of her hand slapping his cheek before she resumed kissing his face. 'Don't you *ever* scare me like that again, okay?'

'Sorry, princess,' he whispered, his voice still raspy.

She pulled her face back, searching his eyes, her eyebrows pulled together and a smile tugging at her lips. He reached his hand up to cup her cheek and pulled her closer to kiss her tenderly. When they broke the kiss, he had only one thing left to say.

'I love you, too, Caitlyn.'

Her head jerked back, her eyes wide. 'You heard that?' He nodded. 'God, I thought I'd lost you,' she said, her eyes tearing again.

'You know, you were the last thing I saw.' He tucked a stray hair behind her delicate ear. 'You, in all of your beauty. And we sat on the park bench. *Our* park bench. And we talked about how we were meant to be.'

'Axel,' she started.

'I can't lose you, Caitlyn,' he said. 'I've lost so much in my life, but I can't lose you. Promise me, please.'

She nodded, pressing her lips against his again. 'Okay.' She tucked her chin, resting her forehead against his. 'I love you.'

He couldn't fight the smile, nor did he want to. 'Those words brought me back, Caitlyn. *You* brought me back.' He patted the bed next to him and she sat, leaning against his good arm.

'You know,' she said, smiling. 'I had a surprise date planned for you. We were going to have a homecooked meal by candlelight and you might have got some, if you were lucky.'

'I'm sorry I missed it,' he said, kissing the top of her head. 'Wait, you cooked?' She nodded. 'Don't tell me—'

'Lasagne,' she teased.

'No!'

She laughed. 'I put it in the fridge, but it'll probably be ruined by the time you come home.'

'Darling, I would eat it out of the rubbish bin if I had to,' he said, pulling her close.

She slapped his good arm. 'Well, hopefully it doesn't come to that.'

'I'll make it up to you,' he whispered into her hair.

'Will you do yoga with me?' she teased. 'I bet that down-doggie pose would *really* help with your recovery.'

His lips pulled into a grin. 'You planned this, didn't you?' He held her hand between his, studying her slim fingers.

'Never!' she said defensively. 'I'm just an opportunist.'

And so was he. He didn't care how long they'd known each other. He felt as though he'd known her his whole life. And a beautiful hand like hers deserved a beautiful ring on it sooner rather than later. And he knew of a good courthouse in town to get it done. He would never forget the time he found his bride on the park bench, and he would always know that it was more than just a coincidence.

It was fate.

Written in the Sand

Turn over for a sneak peek at the next in the series by

R.J. Groves

Chapter 1

There was a word for it. A word to describe something like this—when you're not sure if you're heartbroken, devastated, relieved, or just don't know how the hell you feel. When you're yet to shed a tear and feel like a fool for not seeing it coming.

Empty.

That's what she felt. It's also what her glass was. *Empty.*

Wren waved her hand to catch the bartender's attention, not taking her eyes off the bench. Her left hand still had the imprint of where her ring used to sit—a tan line determined to remind her of this day for the rest of her life.

'Another one, sweetheart?'

'Do you have to ask?'

She nudged her glass closer to the bartender and watched as he poured a shot of the amber liquid into her glass. He reached under the bench and pulled out a small bowl of mixed nuts, placing it in front of her.

'Eat something.'

He moved to the other end of the bar to serve another lonely soul, leaving her to think in peace. Just her, her drink, and a bowl of nuts. She scrunched her nose up at the bowl of nuts and pushed it to the side. She wasn't one to eat food with the same name as inappropriate body parts or anything that resembled them in any way. Nuts were out. And kiwi fruit was out just for looking like one.

She took a sip of her scotch, the smooth woody texture rolling around in her mouth before leaving a trail of fire down her throat and into her stomach. Already, she felt the mellowing effect. She swallowed the lump in her throat. She would *not* cry. She would *not* shed a tear for that asshole. She wouldn't give him the satisfaction. But to be honest, he probably didn't care. He'd played her like a fool and tossed her to the curb.

But she should have seen it coming. She was good at predicting outcomes. She was a social media marketer, with six years of experience in her marketing career. She was good at seeing what would come out of a situation. But this? She hadn't seen *this* coming. Maybe if she hadn't been so caught up on the whole plan of being married by the time she was thirty, she might have seen the signs.

And maybe that's why she wasn't so hung up on him. Sure, she was disappointed—disappointed that she would be thirty next year and no prospective husband in sight, that is—but she wasn't devastated. She wasn't heartbroken over him. Looking back on it, there really wasn't anything there. There couldn't have been. Not when she wasn't what he was interested in.

At least the rest of her life was on track. She had a nice nest egg of savings, a car that ran, a nice apartment with semi-affordable rent, and a good job. Well, the job was only going to get better. She'd been working her ass off for three years to line herself up for the marketing manager position. And now, there was actually a position available and her boss, Hans Durgan, knew that she wanted it. If anything, he'd made more hoops for her to jump through to prove her worthiness for the job. It was only a matter of time before he announced who the next marketing manager would be. But God, she was not a patient woman.

She downed the remainder of her scotch, shutting her eyes tightly as it burned down her throat. She wasn't one to drink those fruity or sweet drinks. Scotch was sophisticated. It was sharp and smooth at the same time. It didn't need to be mixed with anything to taste good. It practically represented her—sophisticated, sharp, independent. Her eyes still closed, she placed the empty glass back on the bar, and rested on her elbows. She heard a stirring in the pub behind her—a heated dispute of some kind—and she heard the bartender's raised voice moving towards the ruckus to break it up. But she wasn't bothered. In a few moments, they would calm down or at least take it outside where it wouldn't disturb her.

'You know, a scotch drinker would know that scotch should be savoured, not downed in one go.'

Her eyes shot open and she stared into eyes the colour of grey marble that flashed with amusement. She examined the features sporting the eyes— tussled ash brown hair that was a couple inches long, slightly tanned skin, a defined square jaw with the best damn three-day growth she'd ever seen, and lips curved into a mischievous grin that made her heart skip a beat. He was resting on his elbows on the bar, so he was level with her, his broad shoulders and biceps bulging underneath his black tight-fitting shirt.

'Ahh,' she said, regaining her composure. 'But a *true* scotch drinker knows that the first drink is to be savoured, and the rest to get drunk.'

'And who said that?'

'I did.' She pushed her glass towards him. 'Hit me.'

His grin widened as he pushed off the bench with his hands and grabbed the bottle from behind him. She took a moment while he wasn't looking to appreciate his masculine back and very defined ass and legs that his jeans fit snugly. Hey, she was back on the market now, right? She could look at whoever the hell she pleased. He placed a fresh glass next to hers and poured a shot into each of them. He nudged hers back towards her and raised the other one in a toast.

'To getting drunk,' he said.

She clinked her glass against his and they both downed the liquid. He poured another shot into their glasses and put the bottle back on the shelf.

'So, tell me what we're celebrating,' he said.

***

Nate had just finished his last shift at the pub when he saw her take a seat at the bar. Wavy chin-length hair the colour of champagne, a body that made any man take a second glance at her, and dressed in a black knee-length skirt, white buttoned shirt, and a navy-blue jacket that was long enough to cover her ass—it near on pulled him towards her. From the other end of the bar, he'd watched her drink her first drink slowly—twelve-year-old single malt scotch whisky—and watched as she downed the second drink. He liked a woman who could handle her whisky. But he hadn't expected her to drink it like it was a shot. When he saw Russ—his best friend and now ex-colleague—move towards the ruckus at the back of the room, he took his chance to meet this intriguing woman who caught his eye.

She was even better up close.

Beautiful couldn't even begin to describe what she was. The way her long eyelashes had rested against her cheeks when he'd come over to her, her striking eyes that were like looking into the deep blue of the ocean, the soothing tone of her voice as she countered his remark, the look she gave him when she wanted another drink. She was something. She was enough to make a man's mind run in circles and have him at her mercy. She was the most incredible creature he'd ever laid eyes on.

'I'm supposed to be getting married tomorrow,' she replied, her eyebrow raised into a perfect arc, examining the glass between her hands.

Her answer felt like a knife being pushed through his chest. He'd been selective with women—always had been. He wanted to be the kind of guy who'd treat a woman right. Sure, he'd had a couple of one-night stands in the past and been on a few bad first dates. But he always had one rule: he would never get involved with someone who was already in a relationship. That was guaranteed to get messy. But something about this woman made him want to forget any rule he ever had.

His eyes dropped to her left hand. There was a faint line where a ring used to sit, but no ring. Then, he realised that she hadn't said that she *was* getting married tomorrow.

'What happened?' he urged.

She sighed. 'He decided it would be a good idea to elope, instead.'

'I take it you didn't?'

Her other eyebrow joined the one that was already raised. 'Oh, I didn't. He did.'

Nate shook his head slowly, squinting, questioning. Was this going to be one of those cliché he-ran-off-with-my-best-friend stories he'd heard so many times in his years of working at the bar?

'With a man,' she finished, taking a sip of her scotch while it sunk in.

'Oh.'

Oh. So, a bit of a different twist to the cliché story he'd heard. But God, wouldn't the guy have worked it out before getting engaged and planning a wedding with someone he's not even interested in?

She let out a breath. 'Yeah,' she said, twirling the glass between her hands again. 'I really should have seen it coming though. I mean, he used to fix up my outfits and my hair and makeup. He had a real knack for anything design.' She shook her head. 'I should have suspected it when I realised he knew more colours than I did.'

'Why didn't you?'

She shrugged. 'I guess I was just caught up in the whole plan to be married by the time I'm thirty.' She leaned back spreading her arms to the side, her top few buttons that were undone granting him a glimpse of her cleavage. 'But here I am—almost thirty and I got stood up by a gay guy.' She dropped her gaze into her lap. 'Show's how good my taste in men is.'

'Well, he's a bastard for leading you on. But I'm sorry it didn't work out,' he said, though he knew he was lying. If anything, he was grateful it didn't work out. It gave him a chance to meet her. That wasn't selfish, right?

'It's not your fault,' she said, fluttering her eyelashes at him. 'At least my career is more promising than my love life. I'm due for a promotion, so that should keep my mind busy.'

'What do you do?'

'I'm a social media marketing manager for now,' she said, her eyes flashing. 'But I'm hoping that will change soon enough. I've waited too long for it.'

'I'm sure you'll get it,' he said. 'You do drink scotch, after all. My bets are you'd have it over any other person you're up against.'

'Just because I drink scotch?' Her eyes were questioning, challenging.

He nodded. 'What you drink says a lot about you.'

'And what *does* it say about me?' She was leaning on her elbows, her hands propped under her chin. He had a better view of her cleavage, and he struggled to hold onto his train of thought.

'Well, scotch is a sophisticated drink,' he started, leaning on his own elbows, and trying to keep his gaze from dropping away from her eyes. 'It has a certain distinction to it and would often be thought as a manly drink. But a woman who drinks it—she's strong, independent, always up for a challenge, gets the job done, and doesn't let anything get her down.'

Her mouth dropped open slightly, and he could see her jaw moving slightly as if trying to say something but not quite getting it out. Her head tilted to the side, examining him. Then, her lips curved into a smile.

'It says all that?' she said. He was sure he caught a flirty tone in her voice.

He nodded, a smile of his own spreading across his face. Who was this woman? And why the hell was he so drawn to her that he was doing stupid things? Like standing behind the bar he no longer worked at, serving drinks to a pretty woman sitting by herself. He heard a throat clear and turned to see Russ standing next to him, his arms crossed over his chest.

'Have you forgotten you don't work here anymore, Nate?'

He slapped his hand on Russ's shoulder. 'Just filling in for you while you dealt with'—he waved his hand in the direction of where the fight was—'that. I couldn't let this lovely lady wait for her drink, could I?'

'You know the rules. Staff only behind the bar.' Russ pointed across the bar. 'Move it.'

'Aww, don't be like that, Russ,' Nate said. He spread his arms out to the side. 'What if my life depended on it?'

'It doesn't. But my *job* depends on it.'

'Wait, you don't work here?' She was staring straight at him, the flash in her eyes somewhere between surprise and amusement.

'Oh, no, I did. I just finished my last shift,' he said. 'Russ is just sad because I'm leaving him.'

'You've already been replaced, Nate, by someone much prettier than you.' Wow, they moved quick. He liked to think he was a little more … irreplaceable. 'Now, before every man and his dog wants to come behind the bar.' He shook his hand to emphasise that he was still pointing across the bar.

He glanced at the woman at the bar, still very much amused with the interaction, plucked the half-empty bottle of scotch from the shelf, and slid across the bar, somehow landing himself next to the woman.

'I hope you're going to pay for that,' Russ said, his arms crossed again, his head shaking slowly.

'Take it out of my last paycheck,' he said, winking. He reached his hand out towards the woman who'd caught his eye. 'Shall we?'

He wasn't sure if he'd been expecting her to take his hand or not, but when he felt the warmth of her hand in his and the shock it sent through his body, he was glad that she did.

Books by R. J. Groves

The Bridal Shop series
Save the Date
Be My Valentine
Say You'll Be Mine

Jilted Brides series
Finding a Bride
Written in the Sand

Cities of the World series
In Paris
The Irish Maiden

Set Ups series
The Set Up

Mail Order Brides series
The Calm in the Storm
The Warmth in the Winter
The Song in the Silence

Standalones
Writing You
Two Babies Too Many
Second Chance
The Boyfriend Application
Sweeter Things
Home Bound
Stay With Me
Her First Noel
When Dreams Come True
To Fall For You

Thank you for reading!
I hope you enjoyed this
story as much as I did
writing it.
R. J. xx

9 780064 526756 3